LOVED BY THE MAFIA KING

MAFIA KINGS
BOOK TWO

BELLA MOONDRAGON

For my Family

CONTENTS

A HUGE MESS TO CLEAN UP

Eleni

I STARE out of the wide window in the bedroom I used to share with Mama over the Narrows. The setting sun glints off the water, and my heartbeat pounds slowly in my ears. I don't remember coming back to Staten Island. I don't know if someone drove me, or I drove myself, or if I walked.

I changed at some point into a soft dress. Dante's blood remains on my hands. Other than that, all I know is this view, my heartbeat in my ears, and the uncertain sense that everything has changed.

Dante is in a hospital somewhere. *I think.* Or he's dead in the back of an ambulance or the doctor's car. That knowledge washes over me numbly. An hour ago—a day ago, it would have rocked me to my core. *Torn me apart.* There's a real chance I'll never look into Dante's dark eyes and see love looking back at me again. I am alone in America. But in the wake of what he said, I can't shake the feeling I was alone in America already.

Christos is dead. That does ache. As much as I thought Luca killed him, part of me still hoped he was just hidden away in some basement, toiling until he got the chance to return to us. I didn't even get the chance to ask where Dante abandoned his body before the doctor rushed him away. Without conscious thought, I turn and leave the room, walk down the hallway until I reach Dante's door. It's closed. Dimly, I remember the threats not to enter without him, the intensity in his eyes. Was he hiding the manacles on his bed? The pictures? Or something worse?

I open the door and drift over to the wall of pictures. He didn't move the one of him and Christos. Did he trust me? Or was he just laughing at me behind my back? I pluck the picture off the wall and stare at it. How could I not have known Christos had fallen into this mafia mess? In the last year, after he dropped out of college, he was a little withdrawn, a little more snappish. Mama said that was because he was having a hard time figuring out what to do with his life. She said to give him space.

In the hollow of my chest, a small flame of frustration lights. That space may very well have been the thing that killed him. None of us knew. And I'd think getting involved with the mafia would be a difficult, obvious process.

Unless the mafia smiled at you and asked your favorite memory of gyros.

I shake my head. That's…different. Right?

Somehow, I find myself wanting to know more about what happened between them. How they went from brothers in arms to enemies on opposite sides of a war. I leave Dante's room. My footsteps echo on the wood floor, another reminder that I'm alone. I could call Mama, tell her it's safe to come home. But she'd ask, and I can't explain it all now. Not through the numbness blanketing my limbs, my tongue.

Do I owe Dante the same vengeance I meted out against Luca?

I open the door to Dante's office. If there are answers to be found in this house, they're in here. If they're not here, I'll bang on the doors to Piacere until they have to let me in and show me the basement I vaguely remember through a haze of alcohol. I'll shake them out of Seb, of Tony. They're somewhere. I just have to look.

Dante's desk beckons. I sit in his leather chair and inhale. His smell filters into my lungs, and something cracks within me. I clutch the picture of Christos so hard the paper crumples.

What am I doing? I'm a twenty-three-year-old waitress with two semesters of night school under my belt. I don't belong here. I only made sense in this world with Dante at my side, and now he's—

Tears sheet down my face. A whirlwind of emotions catches me in its hold, and I slump to the top of the desk, just shaking.

An engine roars up the drive outside, then a second one. Maybe I should just stay here, let whatever loose Lombardi or Coppola soldier find me to end the confusion.

No. Mama and Baba raised me better than that. Calimerises don't give up. I scrub the tears off my face and sit up just as the front door slams open.

"All right, let's whip this place into some kind of fucking shape," Uncle John says, his voice muted by the distance between Dante's office and the front foyer. "Where does Dino keep his papers?"

Someone replies. Maybe several someones. I can't make out the words.

"Because I'm *the fucking boss* now," Uncle John snaps.

"Dante and I have talked about this," Tony says so tightly I imagine him gritting his teeth. "If something happens to him—"

"Look, I love the kid, but you and I both know he's been off his game recently," Uncle John replies with vitriol. "Why don't we just—" He drops his voice lower, and I lose the ability to hear the conversation.

I strain to hear, but I can only make out the tone. Everybody sounds frustrated. Dante keeps a gun in his desk somewhere, I know. I open a drawer and rustle through. Nothing but stationery. The next drawer is all files. Footsteps approach me. This is taking too long. Dante would want his gun fast if he needed it. I run my hands along the underside of the desk and find a leather holster with a pistol.

The door bursts open. Uncle John stands there, with Tony and a few other men behind him.

"What the fuck are you doing behind Dino's desk?" he demands.

"I was—"

"Shut up." His face turns red as he whips around to Tony. "What the fuck is the Greek slut still doing in my nephew's chair? In his fucking house?"

The numbness creeps over me again. Dante's dead. He must be dead.

"Because she was captured earlier today," Tony replies. "And she's a Saint."

"*She's* a—" Uncle John's eyes bulge, and a vein leaps out on his neck. "No. No she's not. She's a fucking mistake you'd be dragging out by her hair if you had the sense God gave a brick." He advances toward me, wild with anger. "She ruined everything. She made Dino ruin everything. I told him, fucking warned him, that he was losing it. Shit, for all we know, she's a Lombardi plant. Wasn't her brother—"

His yelling turns to a roar in my ears that melds with my own heartbeat.

I don't think. I don't feel myself stand and raise the gun. I simply take aim, and fire.

Uncle John falls to the floor, blood splattering out of a hole in the center of his chest. Tony looks from the smoking gun to me, his eyes wide with mingled grief and shock.

I set the pistol down on the desk. The grip bears a bloody handprint as I slowly sit down and clear my throat. "Is everyone ready to get to business now? Because we have a huge mess to clean up."

2

BAD NEWS

Dante

I open my eyes to see a popcorn ceiling overhead. Before I can finish thinking how much I fucking hate popcorn ceilings, a pain like I've never felt before rips through my chest. I grunt and try to twist away from it. My cheek meets a plastic couch cover, and I recoil.

Where the fuck am I?

Glancing around as much as I can without agitating whatever's going on in my chest yields little. Puke-brown walls. The back of the couch I seem to be laying on, a grandmotherly floral print.

Popcorn fucking ceilings. I inhale and smell…soup? Chicken soup, I think, and medicinal alcohol.

None of this makes any goddamn sense, and I feel like shit. My mouth is dry like I got blackout drunk and collapsed in someone's shithole apartment, but I haven't done that since college. Getting that drunk is just offering my enemies an opportunity at this point. But I can't piece enough memories together to come up with another idea.

Finally, I grit my teeth against the pain and lever myself up a little. I nearly puke from how bad it hurts, but a few deep breaths through

5

my nostrils, and I think I'm steady. I open my eyes and look down at myself.

"Holy shit," I mutter.

My chest looks like somebody turned me into Frankenstein, tight black stitches spidering in every direction like railroad tracks. A few staples gleam in my skin. They look medical, for which I'm thankful. My legs seem fine, though I'm wearing a pair of light blue sweatpants I've never seen before in my life. I scrape through my memories for details. Eleni and I met Thano, who betrayed us. A couple of Luca's goons whisked her to a warehouse in Jersey. I followed the beacon from her GPS necklace there. And then….

"Motherfucker." A broad woman with a scowl on her lined face steps into my limited view. "You're going to undo all our hard work. Back to sleep."

"N—"

She grabs my arm and jams a needle into it before I can finish the word. The world goes black around me.

I OPEN my eyes to see a popcorn ceiling overhead. I *fucking hate* popcorn ceilings.

A wave of déjà vu washes through me. I've done this before. But last time…last time, I couldn't see the top of someone's dark hair. And my chest hurt like I'd been hit by a truck. Now, it just hurts like I was hit by a mid-sized sedan. I twist my head to the side to see who's sitting next to me.

Tony, his hair slightly rumpled in a way I know means he's coming apart at the seams, perks up when I move. "Dante! Thank fuck–"

"What the fuck is going on here?"

Tony purses his lips for a second. It's his worst tell. He's got crap news.

"Come on, Tone," I say. "Don't fuck around."

"Luca shot you," he says.

I scowl.

"Then Eleni shot him," he continues. "He's dead."

I exhale slowly. She did it. She got her revenge. I only hope it tasted as sweet as she wanted it to.

"Do I have a prognosis?" I ask.

"Yeah, Poindexter, Domino figures you died last week." Tony rolls his eyes. "You're at his place, by the way. Safer than a hospital. No one knows you're here but me, Dom, and the doctor in our pocket."

My heart skips a beat. "Last week? How long have I been out?"

He purses his lips again. The bastard. "About two weeks."

I drop my head back against the pillow and stare at the fucking ceiling. Two weeks ago, I was shot, and a man called Domino has been storing me on his couch since then. He must've been the one who reconstructed my chest. I owe him for that. More than a standard favor. Shit, a bullet to the chest, I should be six feet under already. But if Tony's confident enough to be an ass, I must be out of the woods. Once I get out of this place, Eleni and I can actually start a life together.

"How are things?" I ask quietly, hoping he'll say fine and that I can hole up with Eleni somewhere to recuperate.

He sighs. "A lot has changed. John is dead."

Well, shit. Uncle John was a dick in the days before I was shot, but I have fond memories of him from when I was younger. Much younger.

"Help me sit up," I say.

Tony squeezes an arm between my shoulders and the pillow, then leans me against the back of the couch. I wince as the pain doubles, but I don't make a noise.

"Gonna have to get you a wheelchair at this rate," he says.

"For keeping me locked up here for two weeks, I might want to start shopping in your size," I mutter. "The sweatpants Domino's too?"

Tony shakes his head. "The wife's. Domino's were too big."

I close my eyes and inhale slowly. "If anyone ever learns that, I'll send a piece of you to your nonna."

"And never taste her lasagna again?" He grins.

I eye Tony for several more seconds as my brain starts to catch up to my body. Two weeks. Two fucking weeks…

A few more pieces of the puzzle fall into place in my mind. Seb, Tony, and I went into the warehouse with backup outside. Luca taunted me, touched Eleni in places that made me see red. I shot first. Then, my memory fizzles out again.

"Is Eleni okay?" I ask.

Tony purses his lips, and disappointment nearly drowns out the pain. She's alive, he wouldn't have hidden that from me, but that face can only mean one thing. She went to Greece. I don't begrudge her that. It doesn't exactly seem like Domino's place has visiting hours. But I begin tallying the calls I need to make to get on the next plane to that little seaside town I know she mentioned at some point and bring her back.

"How much do you remember?" he asks. "From after you got shot?"

What? "Zilch."

Tony nods slowly. "You don't remember Eleni saying she loved you?"

The memory blossoms in my mind like a movie. Dizzying pain, my own ragged breaths, and a bloodstained Eleni leaning over me, saying she loved me. Saying nothing could convince her otherwise. Goosebumps creep over my arms, and I know I don't want to remember the next part. But the movie keeps playing. I sputter nonsense, choke on my own blood, decide I can't keep lying to her. And then I tell her I killed Christos. Her face shutters in my mind's eyes, the second before the memory goes dark.

Fuck.

"I've got some bad news," Tony says, heaving a breath. His expression softens, and he shrugs, looking almost disbelieving as he continues, "A lot has changed."

3

BUSINESS AS USUAL

Eleni

I PULL into the complex of warehouses on the docks in the bright-blue sedan Dante bought me. It arrived a couple days after our run-in with Luca. At first, I was going to ignore it, like the tracking necklace I took off after that first meeting and haven't moved from my nightstand since, but it turns out running a syndicate requires a lot of driving.

Gianna turns up the radio. "Well, I think you're crazy."

I expected her to be furious with me after I shot John. Still, I refused to let Tony give her the news, after all she's done for me. When she hugged me and said it was a long time coming, I asked her to be my right hand. No matter what he said, Tony was still Dante's. And I didn't want anything of Dante's around to make me think of him, even after I found out he was recuperating in hiding.

"No one takes me seriously when I pull up in this thing," I complain. "It's like a neon sign, begging them to treat me like a little girl."

"It's your favorite color!" She leans back against her seat,

9

displaying the fact that she's traded out her usual sports bra and leggings for a fitted skirt-suit in deep purple. "I'm not giving up color." Her playful smirk almost brings a coy smile to my own mouth, but I don't know if I remember how to smile.

I don't remember how to feel, honestly. The only thing I feel, the only thing remotely recognizable, is that aching, desperate numbness that has had me in a chokehold for fifteen days.

I turn back to the gravel parking lot and set my expression to cold, hard steel.

We pull up to the warehouse. Three capos stand with the foreman, waiting for Gianna and I to begin the meeting. The foreman looks the car over, long and slow, then snickers.

"Yeah, I'm painting it." I switch off the vehicle and get out.

Gianna joins me, and together, we stride through the salty air up to the four men. One of the capos, Armando, wordlessly hands me a clipboard. I take it and study the shipping manifest on the front. Luxury car brands dance across the page, blurring in front of my eyes. I haven't slept more than twenty minutes in…long enough that I've stopped keeping track. Falling asleep just gives my subconscious permission to play memories of the good weeks I spent with Dante, and I won't let it remind me of him either.

"These quantities aren't right," I say.

Armando frowns. "What? I thought—"

I point to a line on the second page. "The total number of cars is what I was promised, but they're being shipped to the wrong locations. Forty to Germany, a hundred and seven to Kazakhstan? Does that sound right to you?"

"Let me see that." The foreman holds his hand out for the clipboard.

Gianna scoffs and looks him up and down. "Why?"

He pales. "I just want to check—"

"What, that she's not stupid?" Gianna crosses her arms. "Her title vouches for that. Fix the fucking quantities."

Armando smirks at the foreman and shrugs, looking smug as hell.

I'm sure this is a sight to see—me in my tailored Armani suit with my baby blue SUV sparkling in the background.

Yet I'm the boss right now. And everyone in the Saints knows it.

The foreman opens and closes his mouth a few times, then turns and marches back into the warehouse. I shoot Gianna a thin smile. It's all I can muster. I asked her to help me because I needed someone to side with me, but it turned out she has a way with not just the capos, but every other man who thinks they can talk down to us. I want to be grateful to her, but gratefulness is yet another emotion I've let slip through my fingers over the past couple weeks. The numbness that swallowed me up when I shot John hasn't faded. I haven't let it.

Shooting John was the catalyst to a series of events I hadn't been prepared for. The Staten Island Saints needed a leader in the interim, and as much as Dante apparently promised the role to Tony, I realized very quickly that he gets pissy if he has to sit around in the office for too long. The Saints are better off with him on the streets cleaning up the Lombardi and Coppola stragglers, and me here doing whatever this is, and to my surprise, Tony agreed.

So, I'm running the show, no matter what that means for my emotions. I'll deal with them later when Dante comes back and I can just... go away and forget any of this ever happened to me.

I flip through the next couple pages on the clipboard. This warehouse is handling a shipment of electronics this week as well, all headed into Russia after a recent jump in tariffs. I'll have to talk to the customs people before we leave. It's bigger than our usual orders, and security around Russia is tighter than most.

As I turn to the final page, I realize I'm better off this way. I can still remember how I used to be, a leaf in the storm of my emotions, chasing my heart wherever it led me. Well, it led me to Dante, and he killed my fucking brother. More than that, I used to be a waitress with dreams of maybe computer programming someday. Now, I have hundreds of people more or less ready to jump when I snap my fingers. And with Gianna at my side, they'll be readier and readier as time goes on.

The skills from programming carry over to leading a syndicate more easily than I would've guessed. I knew the order was going to have a mistake before I even left today because the foreman uploaded his reports, so I set up a simple script to scan for discrepancies. Organizing men is the same way. Tony gave me a rundown of everyone's strengths and weaknesses when I stepped up, and I have a program to sort through them all and select the best guys for the job. Really, I'm stronger, smarter, and tougher than I used to be. Maybe I ought to thank Dante.

But I'll never be innocent, joyful, loving Eleni Calimeris again. She's gone. She died, I realize, the day I watched my dad get killed, I just didn't know it yet.

A black sedan skids to a stop in front of the warehouse, and I whip around, putting my hand on the pistol holstered beneath my jacket. It doesn't look like a plainclothes cop car, something I learned to recognize back at the Greek Corner for the poker game Baba played once a month. Still, this gun isn't registered, and neither am I. The fewer questions, the better. The passenger's side door opens before the car even shuts off.

Dante stiffly climbs out.

My breath catches. Something flickers in my icy heart. He's wearing most of one of his suits, though the shirt isn't tucked in. It seems to bulge over his chest, like he's still covered in bandages. I rub my fingers against my palms, remembering the sticky feeling of his blood. His dark eyes burn into mine, a furious mixture of emotions, but the rage boiling off his skin is unmistakable.

Gianna and the capos instantly stop talking. Dante rolls like a shadow over the asphalt in front of the warehouse, his eyes never leaving mine. I've spent so many hours falling into those eyes. I don't have the time to waste climbing out anymore.

I look away.

He clears his throat. "Get out. I need to have a word with…Eleni."

I grit my teeth. Of course, the second he can get out of bed, he's the boss again. I brace for the patter of fleeing footsteps.

Nothing. I turn and see the capos and Gianna looking at *me* for permission. A slow smile tugs at my lips.

4

NEW SHERIFF IN TOWN

Eleni

I LINGER in the moment of Dante's capos defaulting to me instead of him, making sure he feels it. Then, I wave my hand.

"Go watch the foreman," I say. "Nothing ranks above making sure the business keeps running."

The capos escape into the building. Behind Dante, the engine shuts off. Gianna raises an eyebrow at me.

"You're good." I smile wryly. "At least if he kills me, we got to shut Piacere down a few times."

Gianna chuckles. "I'm just lucky I know the people who can keep my name off the no-fly list."

"You're just lucky I'm one of them," I say.

It's the most emotion I've let slip into my voice since the shootout.

She sidles around me, and I turn with her to face Dante once again. Tony leans against the outside of the now-quiet sedan he pulled up in, and Gianna joins him. I knew Tony was still Dante's, but if he's sticking around, having my second nearby can't hurt. Finally, I look at

Dante again. Our gazes connecting rings through my limbs like the starting bell of a boxing match.

"Did you hit your fucking head after I got shot?" Dante demands.

The flicker of emotion fades. I square my shoulders. He doesn't get to talk to me like that anymore.

"What, you don't like the suit?" I gesture to one of the many suits I've purchased with his cards in the last two weeks. This one is navy blue with a thin gray pinstripe. I burned the suit I wore to meet Thano, and I haven't bought anything black since.

He stares at me in disbelief. I jingle the glittering chain that stretches between the two silver tips I attached to the collar of my shirt in lieu of a necklace. Gianna said it made me look distinguished.

"You shot Uncle John," he says.

"I thought his face would look better with a bullet in it." I shrug. "I was right, if you're curious."

"You shot him in the chest," Dante spits. "I may have been unconscious, but I have people who keep me in the loop. *My* people, who fucking trust me."

I smile. I knew the capos waiting for me would rattle him. Whatever flickered in my chest is dead and buried, and I'll use the ice that remains to explain to Dante exactly what happened in his absence.

"Is that so?" I take a step closer. "Because I've heard that when bosses go dark for too long, their people start to turn on them. Seek new leadership."

Dante grimaces. "*New* bosses. If you want to play big man on campus, you should get your fucking facts right."

I wave the clipboard dismissively. "It's called learning on the job. There was a sudden opening, no chance to train."

"El"—Dante steps forward wincingly—"you don't have to do this anymore. Just let me handle this."

I laugh. "There wouldn't be anything to handle, if not for me."

Out of the corner of my eye, I watch Tony frown. I'll handle him later.

Dante's temper flares back up as I laugh in his face. "Let me rephrase then: step the fuck down before I have to take my position back!"

There's real heat in his voice, enough that I believe him, if only for a split-second. The truth is, John had some things right about Dante. He has a soft heart. I know he won't touch me.

But I don't know if this new, frozen-solid me won't touch him, and I don't want to find out. I toss the clipboard at his feet.

"Luxury cars tonight. Electronics on Friday." I leave out the tariff hike. If he wants to be the boss so fucking bad, let him figure it out. "And don't worry, I kept your fucking seat warm." I start to storm away.

"El—"

I whip back. "No. My name is *Eleni*. I'm a Staten Island goddamn Saint. And I didn't just keep your seat warm, I shot your uncle in the fucking face to keep him from taking it. Did Tony tell you that?"

Dante grits his teeth.

"Exactly. I've got soldiers scrubbing up the last of the Lombardi operation, too, so you may as well go play a round of fucking golf for all the help you're gonna be in your condition!" I turn on my heel and march to the car, determined not to look back no matter what Dante says.

After a second, Gianna falls into step beside me. My heart hammers in my ears, louder than our heels on the asphalt. What did I just do? How has so much changed so quickly? I thought I loved Dante. I would've done anything for him. And now, he's the bad guy in my story, the asshole who snatches the first thing I'm really good at from my hands. Who killed my brother. The scary thing is that I don't know which of us changed.

He's also a fucking *mafia boss*.

I get into the bright-blue car with Gianna and swallow down a curse. He can't not recognize it. He knows I'm driving the car he bought me, that if he finds his phone—which I locked in the safe in the bottom drawer of his desk after taking all the relevant numbers— he'll be able to track me anywhere.

Gianna remains silent as I throw the car into drive and screech away from the warehouse. Then, she turns down the music and looks at me.

"What?" I snap.

"Are you okay?" she asks.

My heart slams into my throat, frozen and choking. Nobody has asked me that yet. Not since I shot Luca. I blink back—*something* and clutch the steering wheel. Suddenly, I wish I'd gotten a better look at Dante. I saw him wince, but is he actually ready to run the syndicate again? Is he going to hurt himself trying to keep me out? Do I even care? The last two weeks feel like a hazy, distant dream, already slipping through my fingers as the alarm clock blares to wake me up.

"I'm fine," I bite out.

She frowns, but I turn up the music until the windows shake. Of course, I'm fine. I have to be. Because if I'm anything else, the house of cards I've been building since Dante confessed will crumble.

5

SHARDS

Dante

I SLUMP against the passenger's seat, fighting for breath as Tony drives us back through the city streets. Standing up for a few minutes felt like running a goddamn marathon, and I can't forget the burning in my chest anymore. Tony glances at me in the rearview mirror but doesn't say anything. He said enough on the ride over.

As soon as he told me Eleni shot Uncle John, I was on my feet. When he told me it was the same day everything went down with Luca, I put together a picture in my head. I expected her to be grieving, just trying to hold the pieces together.

Instead, she doubled her kill count in a single day. The Eleni I met in The Greek Corner, the one who glowed while telling me about the after-hours gyros, would've broken down. That's the Eleni I was racing for when I hurried out of Domino's apartment while his wife yelled for me to lay back down.

But as we drove to the house for a change of clothes and then where Eleni was "working," a new story took shape. A hardened, take-no-shit Eleni who ran the Saints for her own reasons and in her own way. I couldn't believe it.

As Tony turns onto the Verrazano Bridge, part of me still can't. I just keep thinking about her twirling in her suit before we left to go meet Thano, giggly and nervous and waiting for my word. Hell, in the car on the way home from the safe house upstate, when she couldn't name a single goddamn organization.

"Uncle John was trying to take over?" I ask quietly.

Tony shrugs. "I had him handled."

The day I got shot, he was angling for my seat. Maybe Eleni did the right thing, killing him. That thought is so incongruous, it almost makes me laugh. I can't imagine Eleni, my El, with blood on her hands.

"So, she's handling the business," I say. "Keeping the shipments on track."

Tony purses his lips. The next time he does that, I'm knocking the look off his face. Assuming I can ever muster enough energy to move my arms again.

"She was." He stares at the road. "Then, a pocket of Lombardi loyalists popped up."

I closed my eyes. "How many is a pocket?"

"Almost a dozen," he says. "She gave the order, we cleaned it up, and I expected that to be the end, but before we even got to lick our wounds, she called…she says it's an all-hands meeting. Everybody piled in, and she declared open season on anyone who ever ran with the Lombardis or the Coppolas, unless they join the Saints on probation."

I exhaled slowly. I was out for two weeks. With the first pocket, and how big those organizations were…Eleni has to have dozens of deaths on her hands now. That doesn't fit with the polished, put-together woman I'd seen at the docks. She couldn't know what those orders meant. The Eleni I knew wouldn't be able to get out of bed after that many murders, much less run a warehouse with the sort of instinctual precision I'd seen in the capos.

Two weeks, and they were all eating out of her little hands. Maybe I never knew Eleni in the first place.

Tony pulls up to the house. "You want me to...?"

I shake my head. "If I can't walk up my own front stairs, you should just put me down."

He frowns but lets me climb out on my own. Every muscle aches. Exhaustion drags me slower and slower. By the time I reach the front door, I'm puffing like a pack-a-day smoker. It suddenly occurs to me that I don't know if Eleni changed the locks. I pull out the set of keys Tony gave me with shaking hands, leaning on the doorframe for support, and slide the one that should work into the knob. It twists. She hasn't given up on me entirely.

Inside, two armed soldiers stand next to the door. I've never stationed guards inside.

"Go home," I say tiredly.

They exchange looks. Not again.

I straighten up as much as I can manage, my stitches pulling unpleasantly, and put on my old scowl. "Go. Home."

They leave and shut the door behind them. I slump. Am I even still the boss, if my own men won't answer to me? Through my haze of self-pity, I realize the house is silent. No Gianna. No Eleni. I expected them to be here. Hell, I expected them to be in my office. I trudge up the stairs to my room.

The door is ajar. The light is on. I push inside with my heart pounding, imagining any number of enemies sitting on my bed with Eleni's corpse at his feet.

The only things on my bed are a few cardboard boxes labeled "Dante" and a half-packed suitcase. I stare around at the room. My wall of pictures is turned so the other side of the cork faces out, and sticky notes of business terms cover the back. The chains on the bedposts are gone, and my bedspread has been replaced with...is that the quilt from the guest bedroom Eleni was sleeping in? The soft hiss of the shower edges into my notice, then abruptly cuts off. I turn toward the bathroom door and find it open. Eleni finishes wrapping a towel around herself and steps to the sink. She spots me in the mirror.

"Oh," she says quietly, as if to herself. "You're back."

"What are you doing?" I gesture to the boxes on the bed.

She picks up a comb and runs it through her hair. I stare blankly. Her toothbrush wasn't in here when I left. Nothing was. She sleeps down the hall.

"You have the better bathroom." She shrugs. "And I needed my bedroom for an office."

"You know damn well that's not what I'm asking." I start to storm toward her, but pain shoots through me. I grab one of the bedposts for support. "The fucking boxes?"

"The boxes are *stuff* of yours that I moved," she sniffs. "The suitcase is mine. We're even, so I'm leaving."

I blink. My chest aches in a new way, which at least adds some novelty to what is quickly becoming the worst day of my life. "Even?"

"You killed Christos. I killed John. We're done here." She meets my gaze in the mirror, and her eyes are dead. Completely emotionless.

Anger flushes my veins. This is still my house, still my syndicate, until they put me in the goddamn ground. Whatever is happening between Eleni and I will be done when I say it's done.

My gaze catches on the way her fingers tremble around the comb. Another moment passes, and she bites her lip like she's holding something back. Maybe that's a single sliver of the Eleni I knew.

I will myself to drop to my knees, to beg her forgiveness, to ask her to stay and help run the syndicate while we figure out how to piece back together the shards of what we had. But it's my house. My syndicate. Pride keeps me on my feet.

"You did a good job," I say stiffly. "While I was...out."

Eleni closes her eyes and sets down the comb. "I'm going to go sleep in one of the guest rooms."

She breezes past me on her way out of the room, and it takes every ounce of self-control I have left not to touch her. The feel of her skin is burned into my brain, but I don't want to be screamed at. I'm bone-deep tired of fighting. I turn back to my bed, to the boxes and suitcases I can't lift in my condition, and fish out a pair of pajamas before leaving as well.

Her scent is all over my room, embedded in the sheets. I'm instantly comforted by it, slipping into a hazy half-sleep fractured by stress and conflicting feelings.

Did she sleep here because she found the same comfort in my scent? Did she lay here like I am and realize the slippery slope we're on, and how deep she's fallen, and how much there's left to lose?

I roll over onto my side, staring at the picture-plastered wall.

Maybe it's better if Eleni leaves.

6

CUT OUT FOR THIS

Eleni

THE NEXT MORNING, I wake up on a wide, soft mattress and immediately reach for where I've been plugging my phone in, on my right. My hand swipes through empty air.

Right. Fuck. Dante came home last night and took his room back. Since I moved the bed frame out of my old bedroom to make my office, I couldn't even sleep there. I'm just somewhere in his massive house.

I scrub my eyes and sit up. My laptop shifts on the end of the bed, and I sigh. I stayed up late last night as usual, and now the red eye flight I have planned is going to suck. I climb out of bed, drop my laptop in my office, and head downstairs to make coffee. No point in changing out of the thin, oversized T-shirt I've been wearing to bed. I have nothing to hide from Dante, and he's the only one here.

The coffeemaker dings as I set foot on the first level. He must've woken up before me. I'll just grab a cup and go. There's nothing left to talk about. Just a few hours of packing, and then I'm on my way back to Mama. Hopefully, somewhere over the Atlantic, my chest will stop aching when I think that.

I turn into the kitchen and stop dead. That's not Dante at the coffeemaker, that's Tony. I cross my arms over my chest.

"Uh, hi?" I say.

He turns slowly. "Hey. I made enough coffee for at least a couple more cups."

I study his face for a hint of sarcasm. Ever since I told him I could handle the hot seat and put him back on the streets, he's been avoiding me like the plague. What is he doing now, adding milk to his coffee without a care in the world?

"Thanks." I pour myself a mug and drink it black, like I've started to in the last few weeks. It still tastes completely awful, but I can suppress the grimace now, and nothing else wakes me up the same. "So, uh…what are you doing here?"

Tony leans against the island. "Are you leaving now that Dante's back?"

I blink. I've never heard Tony go so long without a sarcastic comment. I've never spent this long alone with him, actually. Our conversations over the last two weeks have been brief, with me telling him what needs to happen and him saying something along the lines of, "Yes," or "Sure."

"Yeah," I say. "I've got a ticket to Greece on the 10pm out of JFK."

He nods. I look away, reminding myself I don't care what he thinks. I used my own money—well, the cash Dante paid for me that first night at the auction, but really, it's mine. I figure I'll go to Greece, reunite with Mama, and that'll give us the chance to make a new start on our own. It doesn't matter that those daydreams used to feature Dante alongside me. I don't need him, and I don't really need New York.

Plus, I can't keep living here, and there's nowhere else for me to go.

"Don't," Tony says.

I choke on a laugh, certain he must be joking. When he doesn't join in, I peer at him. Once again, no humor in his face.

"You don't even like me." I swig my coffee, hoping I can get enough caffeine into my system that this makes any sense.

He shrugs. "I don't know if that matters."

Great. A confirmation he never liked me. That's what I needed this morning. I'm not why it hurts.

I suck down more black coffee and wonder if I shouldn't switch to those energy drinks.

No. I'm going to Greece with Mama. I don't have a syndicate to keep up with anymore.

When I don't answer, Tony sets his mug down and crosses his arms. "You're good for him. I didn't even realize how bad things had gotten."

I remind myself I don't care about Dante. "Bad how?"

A smile ghosts across Tony's face, and I barely resist the urge to knock it back off. He doesn't know anything about me.

"I mean...I knew Dante through college. He was the king of every party, the center of attention." Tony shakes his head. "Couldn't walk five fucking feet next to him without someone stopping us to say hey and invite him fucking somewhere."

I stare into my mug. That doesn't sound anything like the Dante I met. But I can see snippets of it. In the quiet moments, when we were alone, I can picture him as someone people loved.

"Did you know he used to be the funny one?" Tony asks.

"Used to be?" I retort.

Tony scoffs. "He made people laugh 'til they cried."

He did that to me once. A little more of the ice around my heart chips away, and I scramble to put it back. I need to keep it together until the air hostess is bringing around the little bags of peanuts. Then, I can fall apart.

Tony doesn't care for my timeline. "When his dad died, when he took over, he lost that. And since you've been around"—he shakes his head—"I don't get it, but I see it in him again."

I turn away from him. "Even if I believe you, Dante and I have both done...unforgivable things. Even if I could stay, there's nothing left for us."

"Bullshit." Tony intrudes back into my line of sight. "John was trying to steal the Saints out from under him. He'd been sniffing around for an opening ever since he got out of jail. If you hadn't killed him, I would have before long."

"That doesn't make John *not* family," I mutter. I killed Dante's uncle. That's the truth of it. I shot his uncle and killed him without a moment of hesitation and it felt good, which is the worst part about it. I hadn't felt a lick of remorse for taking his life. Not for a second.

Maybe that's what's been eating away at me lately.

"We're all family in this game." Tony shakes his head. "What you did...that's how people become capos. How they become bosses."

I stare up into his ice-blue eyes. They hold none of the warmth Dante's used to, but I can see the same certainty. Whatever else Tony thinks of me, he believes this.

"I don't care," I say with effort. "I have my own life to lead." I've just gotten it, and I'm not giving it up for the nonexistent hope I can forgive Dante someday. I don't want to.

But a little voice in the back of my head nags that I was good at this. That I enjoyed it.

"You're good at this," Tony says finally. "And I don't tell people that. But you've crushed any future Lombardi problems, knocked the Coppolas into line, whipped our sorry asses into shape." He pauses. "Even Dante admitted it was impressive."

My chest squeezes. I don't care, don't care, don't care! These tears are... are from drinking my coffee too hot, nothing else. I swig more as if to prove it.

Tony's phone rings, and he checks the caller ID.

"Shit. Don't go anywhere, okay?"

I don't reply. He walks away, picking up the call as he does. There is nothing here for me. Not Dante, and not his Saints. I know that. I just don't know why I can't leave the kitchen, like I'm actually waiting for Tony to come back.

My phone vibrates in my hand, and I glance at it. An email from Professor Calhoun about my final. I laugh to myself. I haven't even thought about school since Luca kidnapped me. Finding out I failed my final would be the perfect icing on the cake.

I open the email.

7

CHECKING HER WORK

Dante

I WAKE up in a third-string guest bedroom already pissed. The sun is coming in at an angle that tells me I've already slept later than I meant to, but my alarm clock is in my fucking room, which was too covered in crap to sleep in.

Today is the day Eleni's leaving. She made it very clear she doesn't want anything else to do with me, and I'm inclined to give her that. The woman who marched out of my bedroom last night was someone I'd never seen before. I thought, for a split second, that I could still find Eleni underneath, but I think she died with Luca at that warehouse.

Domino's wife told me I should still spend most of my days resting, but if I lay around anymore, I'm going to get bedsores. I shuffle out of bed, gritting my teeth against the nearly overwhelming pain in my chest, and head down the hall toward my bedroom. I couldn't carry more than one set of clothes last night, and like an idiot, I picked pajamas.

I pass the door to Eleni's bedroom. Slightly ajar. A little of my frustration burns off as I consider that she might already be gone. That I might have had my last conversation with her and not even known it. I still can't imagine a future without her.

I hobble a couple steps forward and push open the door, smiling at the memory of her arguing my door was open on that first night I found her in my room. At least, if she is here, I'll have a good argument.

Inside, the room has been transformed. The bed that used to cover most of the floor was removed, leaving a wide-open space that Eleni seems to have immediately begun making use of.

A desk I don't recognize dominates the space now, a beautiful, light-wood one with a rolling top, behind which sits one of the dining room chairs. Guns hang in neat rows on one wall, and a massive array of sticky notes spirals across the other.

I drift over to the sticky notes first. The logic takes some time to figure out, but soon, I realize I'm looking at a map of all of New York City's organized crime.

Names, relationships, years of history, all splattered across the tan I never repainted because I doubted anyone would care.

I trace the lines, looking for the Saints, and finally find us off to the side. It's offensive until I realize it's a literal map as well as a figurative one. She's painted the city on my walls in vivid color, and I study it like it's the inside of her brain, holding all the secrets I've been trying to pry out.

One of the notes has a circle on it in red. I pluck it off the wall, and my eyebrows shoot up. This one holds a brief, scribbled history of Cal Duncan, leader of the Irish Kings. What the hell is Eleni thinking? The Kings are almost as insane as the Russians. I wouldn't fuck with them without a gun to my head, and if the circle's anything to go by, they're her next target.

I put the note back where I found it. She's not my Eleni anymore. She's someone I don't know, someone who wouldn't flinch from the fucking Irish Kings. She's better off leaving. I'm at fault for creating this monster. I turn to go.

Her laptop sits open on the desktop, like she was in here not long ago. I can see her email client, and one message open with a blinking cursor in the response line. Curiosity gets the better of me. I walk over and scan the screen.

Dear Ms. Calimeris,

Since you weren't in class when grades were given out, I'm taking the liberty of emailing you to let you know you not only scored 100% on the final, but that I found your work exemplary. Your transcript says this is your first year formal schooling, and that you'd done a little coding at home before joining us. Frankly, that's astounding. Your code shows an intuition most IT professionals have to work for years to develop. I don't know what's caused your prolonged absence, but it's a waste of your talent and skill to return to community college, as much as I'll miss you. In that vein, I've taken the liberty of forwarding a small portfolio of class projects to a friend of mine at NYU's Tandon School of Engineering. I think you'd make a brilliant software engineer, and I'd be honored to say it was I who discovered you. Please reply whenever you get a chance. I look forward to seeing where your career goes, whatever you choose.

Best,

Professor Calhoun

My tattered chest aches with pride. She was so worried about failing, and she's good enough that her professor contacted someone at NYU? I always knew Eleni was smart.

And if she's looking at this email, if she's thinking about it, maybe she's thinking about staying. Maybe if she gets out of this life, she can find her old self again.

Someone clears their throat in the doorway. I jerk my head up to see Eleni, clutching a mug and wearing a crisp gray suit.

"What are you doing?" she asks. Her dark, thick hair is pulled back away from her face and she's wearing makeup. She looks different. Beautiful, but different.

I open my mouth with no idea what I'm about to say, and nothing comes out. If I say I was proud, she'll kill me on the spot. If I say I was curious, she'll accuse me of not believing her. If I tell her I still love her and miss her—

"Why did you step up?" I ask.

She clenches her jaw. Wrong question.

"I just mean…Tony and I talked about this." I circle around the desk, trying to hide how heavily I'm leaning on it. "He was ready."

"No, he wasn't," she says quickly.

I raise an eyebrow, and she shakes her head.

"I guess I just didn't know what else to do," she says finally. "Dante, I needed something to do while you were…I'll get this packed up before I leave tonight." She bites her lip.

The words hit like a punch to the gut. I hobble out a little quicker. She steps in behind me, and I can sense her about to close the door. I can't just leave like this, if it really is our last conversation.

I turn back. She is visible only through the remaining crack in the door.

"You should go to Tandon," I say.

Her smile twists under the weight of emotion. "Why? There's nothing left for me in New York."

8

BEEN REAL

Eleni

THAT NIGHT, I stride into Piacere half an hour before Gianna's shift. I've been avoiding her all day because I think she's the only one with a chance of talking me out of this.

Half an hour shouldn't be long enough, though, and I made sure one of Gianna's favorite customers was here tonight, to keep her from delaying her shift to talk to me. It's funny coming back here, though, especially alone.

The first time I walked through these doors, I had no idea what they were going to mean to me. I had to beg my way past the bouncer instead of nodding and greeting him by name. I had to look around like a lost duckling instead of marching to the back, where I know the strippers' dressing room is. I didn't even know what scotch tasted like.

Now, I don't think I'll ever drink scotch again.

I push into the dressing room. Two of the other dancers, Sabrina and Crystal, sit at the mirrors already in costume.

"Hey guys," I say.

33

"Hi, Eleni," they chorus.

Crystal turns to face me and jiggles her chest. "What do you think of the new top?"

I study it. She tends to lean into the literal interpretation of her name, coating herself in what look like real jewels, and the tiny bra she has on tonight is no exception. Glittering strings of red faux-stones drip from the bottom and catch the light when she moves.

"Cute," I say. "With the black dress?"

She leaps out of her seat. "Ugh, you're a genius! I was going to wear the white."

As Crystal races for the racks of costumes, I turn to Sabrina. "Seen Gianna?"

She jerks a thumb at the warm-up room over her shoulder. "Be warned, she's got the music on."

I grimace and head over. Gianna always warms up with music blasting so loud Dante—they had to soundproof the room a few years back.

I open the door, and a guitar riff blares out at me. I lean back like the wall of sound is a physical impediment and try to yell her name over the top. She's at the top of the practice pole right now, holding on by only her legs, so it takes a few shouts before she spirals gracefully down and shuts off the speakers. The silence is almost as startling, after all that noise.

She bounces over to me with a grin, not yet in costume. "What's up?"

"Everything." I sit on the floor with a groan.

"Work stuff?" She drops her voice and joins me immediately.

I shake my head. I knew I shouldn't have come down here in the suit. I only have a couple hours before the flight leaves, and I want Mama to see me looking like an adult. Like I took care of myself without her.

"Try stuff you're not going to like." I lean my head back against the wall so I don't have to look at her.

Gianna goes silent for a long, dangerous moment. "Oh my god, you're letting my idiot cousin chase you away."

"No!" I grimace. "Not really. There's just…nothing here anymore."

"Oh, great." She rolls her eyes. "Good to know where I rank."

"You know I don't mean it like that." I grab her hand. "I'd be a wreck without you."

She leans against my shoulder. "You're a mess *with me*. Why do you want to go to Greece so bad?"

"I didn't say I was going to Greece," I mumble.

Gianna lets another silence refute my disbelief in her. I sigh.

"I miss Mama." That, too, makes something deep inside me hurt. "And…I killed Luca. I got my revenge."

"You don't really expect me to believe you just stayed here for revenge," she replies.

I stare at the opposite wall, where the two of us are reflected back in a long mirror. Gianna keeps saying we look like sisters, but she's only right if we're starring in a comedy. We have almost the same coloring, but she's long and thin everywhere I'm short and with the kind of curves the other dancers cat-call me about often, saying I'd make a killing out on the floor. We look like a mismatched set. But I can't deny how she's kept me afloat these past couple weeks.

"Maybe I don't." I shake my head. "I don't know. Last night, I was dead set. I mean, you saw him. He just screamed at me in front of everyone." I cling to the ice around my heart. "But then Tony cornered me this morning and told me I was good at running the syndicate—"

"—which you are," Gianna interrupts.

"—which *we* are," I correct. "But he's never said that many sentences to me before. And then…I guess there's this." I pull out my phone and show her the email from Professor Calhoun.

Gianna reads for a few seconds, then squeals and throws her arms around me. "Oh my god! My best friend's a freaking genius!"

I hug her back, my heart beating out of time. I've never really had a best friend before. My best friend in school always liked someone else better.

When she finally pulls back, she meets my eyes. "Okay, honest answers only: if Dante wasn't such a shithead, would you leave?"

I dodge her gaze. "I don't have anywhere to stay—"

"Honest. Answers." She grabs my face. "Would you stay?"

I stare into her eyes. Tandon is an incredible opportunity. I know that. And I knew she'd freak if I showed her the email. But as I look at her, see the family resemblance between her and Dante, another unavoidable fact crashes forward.

Dante broke my heart. He killed my brother, he hid that from me, and when he told me, it destroyed everything we had. Tears pile up in my eyes and I struggle to blink them back.

"Oh, honey." Gianna hugs me again, tightly. "Just talk to him. I know he's a shithead, but I don't want you to lose out on things just because he's a shithead. See if there's a way you can stay here, even if you can't forgive him." She squeezes me hard enough to hurt for just a second. "My studio apartment is your studio apartment, okay?"

All my ice, all my numbness is crumbling away. I haven't even told Mama I'm coming yet. I figured I'd text her from the plane, but suddenly, waiting feels like keeping one foot in New York. Like I wanted Gianna to talk me out of this.

"T-minus five, G," Crystal calls.

"I gotta go." Gianna pecks me on both cheeks. "Just think about what I said."

She races off, and I wander back out onto the main floor. At the bar, I think about ordering a rosé, then get a gin martini. I don't think I like these either, but they taste nothing like scotch. As the lights dim, and Crystal takes the stage, I sip the freezing drink.

Just talk to him. I can do that. At the very least, then I'll be able to get on the plane with no regrets.

9

―――――――――

QUEEN OF SAINTS

Dante

I SLIDE into a booth at La Dolce Vita, an Italian restaurant I haven't been to since before Frank Lombardi killed my father and inhale the garlicky air.

"Good, right?" Tony sits next to me. "I've been all over this place the last two weeks."

I shoot him a look. "I've been all over whatever the hell Domino's wife saw fit to feed me. Do you know what that is, by the way?"

"Yeah, I think she prefers a diet of 'shut up, it saved your life,' just like in the old country." Tony picks up a menu. "Are you sure you're ready for this?"

As if to prove his point, my chest burns.

"Yes," I say. "And whether I'm ready or not, I have to get back into the game. She's leaving tonight."

Tony grunts noncommittally, thankfully pulling me away from the attendant ache of that statement.

"What? I thought you'd be throwing her a going away party."

He shrugs just as a waitress walks up to the table.

"What can I get you guys to drink?" she asks.

Tony looks up at her slowly, emphasizing his blue eyes in a move I've seen so many times I can't help but snicker. As always, the woman is too entranced by him to notice.

"What do you suggest?" he asks. "I like to try new things."

She giggles. "Um…I'm new here, so I don't really know. I think we have great wine?"

"Bring us a bottle of your favorite," he says.

She scurries away, and I roll my eyes at him.

"Business, not pleasure," I say.

"You found a way to combine them." He opens his menu.

The door opens, and a few moments later, two men join us. I glance over the top of my menu at them. Ben, the college student who saved Eleni from getting kidnapped with Sebastian sits next to an older, more distinguished version of himself. Exactly who we were waiting for. Our first meeting of several tonight with known Coppola operators.

Ben's old man looks stoic despite the conversation that he knows is about to take place.

"Dante Cattaneo." I stick out my hand to shake. "I don't believe I've had the pleasure."

"Lucio Mazzi." He shakes my hand firmly. "And my son Benicio, whom you know."

I smile at Ben. He just nods, looking tired.

"Tell me how things have been." I gesture broadly, despite the pain in my chest. "I'm paying as long as the story's flowing."

Lucio sighs, and the night begins. We entertain Coppola after Coppola, hearing the same stories of conflict and disorder in the ranks since Thano's death. No, not since Thano's death. Since Eleni called open season. A few of the men we talk to are already technically on Saints' payroll, just on probation, including Ben and Lucio. The Coppola outfit is in tatters. Not everyone knew about the plan to flip on us. Those who didn't feel betrayed. Those who did are terrified of retribution. Everyone is tired of hiding. In a break between meetings, I lean over to Tony.

"I like the father and son," I say.

"For what?" he replies.

I sigh. "We're scooping up all the Coppola territory in the city, and as much of the Lombardi slice as we can. Look at the way these men move around Lucio."

All the Coppola operators loosely circle the end of the bar where Lucio and Ben sit in the unconscious way of men who rely on a leader. After a moment, Tony nods. Lucio is a boss, whether he wants to be or not.

"I see your point. But they're already on probation. What more do you want?"

"Take that off," I say. "Full membership, starting tomorrow, on the ground they'll help us clean up all this confusion."

Tony nods, and I lean back. Finally, I feel a little like my old self again. Maybe I don't need—

Teo, the bartender from Benny's, slides into the booth across from us.

"I thought you were dead," I say mildly.

"Same to you," he replies. "What's this I hear about probationary admittance to the Saints?"

The door at the front of the restaurant bangs open, and I twist as much as I can without wincing. A trio of redheads I don't recognize waltz in.

"Irish Kings," Teo sneers. "They've been hanging around all the Italian spots. Somebody needs to show them the world hasn't ended just because Luca's dead."

I remember the red-circled sticky note. Was this why?

Tony runs his tongue along his lower teeth as he leans into my side and says, "Cal's been making moves on the old Lombardi territory, boss."

Ah, that's why.

The trio of Kings sit right behind us, laughing raucously. I roll up my sleeves. If I'm going to declare that I'm able to run the Saints again, I need to put my money where my mouth is.

Tony grabs my arm in warning, and I freeze. I look slowly up at

Teo, who is staring at Tony's restraining hand. Tony withdraws it slowly and begins rolling up his own sleeves. He knows how the game works. It doesn't matter that I have sutures and staples holding my chest together.

I stand and march to the end of the Kings' table.

"Well, I heard they had some bonny lasses in here, but I never expected the likes of you fine young ladies," I say in an exaggerated Irish accent.

That's all it takes. One of them, the broadest, launches up out of his seat. Mistake. Tony steps out from behind me and slams a fist into his face, immediately knocking him back into the booth. The other two scramble to stand as civilians scream and scatter. A quick glance over my shoulder tells me the Coppola men won't be getting involved. As much as they were auditioning for me, now I'm auditioning for them.

Am I really still the Dante Cattaneo who's run the Saints these past five years?

My chest screams as I snatch a stein of beer off a nearby table and smash it over the head of the second King to find his feet in reply. The smell of hops fills the air, and I suck in a breath just long enough that the third one can land a hell of a right hook on my jaw. I stumble back and catch myself on a chair.

The one who hit me—who has the longest hair of the three by far—crows and leaps forward to hit me again. I swing the chair between us, legs out, and grin as he slams directly into it. One of the legs snaps off, and I abandon the much too heavy seat for the makeshift club. As he struggles to his feet, I smash it into his gut, and he crumples.

"Dante!" Tony shouts.

I whirl to find him on the floor, the other two cornering him. It's as easy as breathing with a bullet in my chest to club the broader one over the head and give Tony enough space to get back up, which he does by slamming his knee into the chest of the smaller one and nearly flipping to his feet. He grabs the wine bottle, shatters it against the table, and brandishes the jagged neck like a knife.

The broader King bellows as he gets to his feet and charges me. I forget all about my injury as I dance to the side at the last second, then bring the chair leg down on the back of his neck. When he falls, I roll him onto his back and bash his teeth in for good measure. By the time I turn back to Tony, the final Irish King has joined his friends in lying on the ground and spitting blood. I pant, feeling alive for the first time in too fucking long.

"Maybe we take the fight outside next time?" Teo looks around at the mess we created, the terrified patrons.

I don't give a fuck about Teo. I bend down to the big King at my feet.

"Tell your boss," I hiss, "that the Staten Island States run New York City, and I'm their fucking *king*."

The man at my feet smiles through broken teeth. "I heard the Saints had a queen these days. Cal's desperate to meet her."

10

———

LAST CHANCE

Eleni

I YANK on the stubborn zipper of my suitcase to no avail. It won't shut. I release with a sigh, and the top flops open to reveal the picture of Dante and Christos I stole from his room. I swallow. I know stealing it is stupid. I don't really know either man in this picture. But it just feels wrong, leaving this image behind in the shadow of what happened here.

I want to remember them like this. Innocent and young, before the Mafia pulled them under.

I don't have any pictures of myself. Mom packed those up and took them with her to Greece. I wonder if I'd even recognize the girl I used to be.

My phone vibrates, and I curse. That's my ten-minute alarm. If I'm not in the car on the way to JFK by the time the last one goes off, I'm going to miss my flight. Gianna convinced me to talk to Dante, but he's making it a hell of a lot harder by not being here. For lack of anything better to do, I grab a pack of the sticky notes I've started going through like water and attempt to write a goodbye note.

43

Dear Dante,

Too formal. I crumple the note and throw it on the ground.

Dante,

Ugh, maybe an introduction is just stilted. I start again.

I'm sorry—

The door opens downstairs, and I throw myself at my suitcase to give it one last try. That has to be Seb, here to pick me up, and the last thing I need right now is him making fun of me as he closes it easily. I can just give him whatever message I was going to write Dante. I guess.

I've just gotten the zipper closed when I hear the thud. Somehow, over the past two weeks, I've learned enough to know that's the sound of a body hitting the ground. I abandon my suitcase and race out of the room, scenarios flying through my head. A pocket of Lombardi soldiers I missed. A couple of Irish Kings, the bastards who have been sniffing around old Lombardi territory. One of the dozens of crews I haven't learned yet.

I don't expect to see Dante lying in the middle of the foyer, spread eagle with his eyes closed. I also don't pause. In seconds, I drop to my knees at his side.

"Dante?" I jostle his shoulder a little.

No response. Oh, god. Like I'm living a memory, I check his body for wounds. His shirt is soaked with blood. I grab on either side of the buttons and tear.

His eyes flutter open. "Skipping foreplay?" His drowsy smile alerts me to the fact he's still alive, at least.

I ignore him. His chest looks like a railway map of stitches, and I can see at least half a dozen that are busted. It's obvious he fell, maybe even off the stairs. Where the hell was he? What was he thinking, two weeks out from a near-lethal shot to the chest? As I look closer, I see more wounds. A bruise blossoming on his chin. Scrapes on his knuckles. He looks like he was in a fucking fight.

"What the hell happened to you?" I snap.

"Fuggin'…redheads…" he mutters.

He's barely lucid. And he reeks of wine and beer, neither of which he really drinks. More blood pools on his chest, and I decide it doesn't matter what happened. I stand and sprint up the stairs for the first aid kit, cursing myself for not keeping one downstairs too. I just need to patch him up enough to get him to a proper doctor. At least I learned a little in the weeks before…whatever we are now.

With the pack in hand, I run back down to his side. "This is going to hurt."

"F-fuck you," he mumbles.

I roll my eyes and pull out the isopropyl alcohol. When I dab some on his skin, he jolts upward in pain.

"Wha—why?"

"I warned you," I say tiredly. "Lay down."

That, at least, he obeys. I pull the broken stitches out of his skin as carefully as I can, though he still swears the whole time. My mind keeps drifting back to my first night in his bed, the first time I tried to patch him up, and I keep yanking it back. I don't need to be thinking those thoughts now. Even as I run my fingers over his scarred skin and map the wound he took to save me.

Staring at the stitches, it's impossible to deny how close he came to death. Dr. Domino is a miracle worker. I find myself thanking him as I work. Whatever else happens, I don't think I want Dante dead.

When all the stitches are out, there's not much else I can do. I haven't nearly practiced enough to try stitching him myself. So, without any better ideas, I start applying little wound-closure strips to the stitches that popped. The rest seem stable enough, and he can get fixed tomorrow. My phone vibrates. Five minutes.

"Seb will be here soon," I say. "I'll have to leave for the airport."

"You're not leavin'," he slurs.

I recoil. "What?"

He grabs my hand, a hazy look in his eyes. "Called Seb. Told 'im… fuck off."

My mouth falls open. Of all the presumptuous, shitheaded things—

"What the fuck do you mean? Why would you do that?" I demand.

His eyes flicker closed again. I finish patching him up and storm to the kitchen for a glass of ice water, intending to throw it on Dante to wake him up. When I return, he blinks up at me and smiles like I'm his favorite person in the world.

Ice. Numbness. I know how to do that.

I don't throw the water on him. I do sit on the stairs a few feet away and seethe while he wakes up properly. Finally, he levers himself up on one arm.

"That's not how I meant to tell you that," he says clearly. He rubs the back of his head and grimaces while glances at the stairs I'm sure he just fell down.

"Fuck off," I reply. "Did you cancel my flight too?"

"We need to talk," he says by way of answer.

I shake my head. "You just hit the floor. You probably have a concussion. Even if I wanted to talk to you, now's a crappy time. God, why would you throw yourself into a fight when you look like you just lost one against a lawnmower?"

"We need to talk," he repeats stubbornly. "About Christos."

"I have—"

He holds up a hand. "And if after that you still want to leave, I'll charter my private plane for you."

I clutch the glass of water and stare at him for a long moment. "Fine."

11

THE TRUTH

Eleni

I STAND BEHIND the chair on the opposite side of Dante's desk and watch him, shirt thankfully buttoned again, ease himself onto the smooth red leather of the boss' seat. Part of me wants to run out of the room before he opens his mouth. I made up my mind. I'm leaving. I don't need to say anything to him other than "goodbye," no matter what Gianna said. But another part of me just keeps thinking of that first day, when I didn't know whether he was alive or dead, and I came down here looking for answers. Anything that could explain why he killed Christos.

He's offering me those answers now. With Mama on the other side of a plane ride to Greece, I would be stupid not to take them. No matter what else, I couldn't face her knowing I could have told her what happened to her baby and refused.

"Sit," Dante says. "Or are you more used to the view from this side of the desk now?"

His smile is an olive branch. He wants to have the conversation peaceably.

I throw myself down in the empty chair across from him. I'd take the olive branch when he earned it.

"Fair enough." He adjusts the ice pack I gave him on the back of his head and straightens. "When I said what I did, I thought I was going to die."

"So did I," I bite out. "What difference does that make?"

"You have to understand that I kept this from you for—"

I scoff. "Kept this from me? That's a funny way of saying you lied for weeks."

"He asked me—"

"I don't care." I kick my feet up on the edge of his desk. "He's not here to answer for whatever he did. You are."

The words burn past my lips. I'm furious, but I haven't really considered whether I'm angry with Christos yet. That seems like a problem I can solve when I'm an ocean away with Mama to dry my tears.

"We can do it like that, if you want." He tosses the ice pack down on the desk with a wince, and his eyes grow hard. "You're a Staten Island Saint, and I killed your brother. I did it for a good goddamn reason, but that doesn't mean I don't owe you answers."

I nod for him to go ahead.

"Everything I told you about Christos is true," he says. "I met him in college, and he was a genius running back. There was an NFL scout at his first game, looking at one of the seniors, and I saw the scout later asking why the hell he hadn't seen number eighty-three on the field before."

I swallow. Christos was so thrilled when he pulled eighty-three. That was the year Mama and Baba met. He said it was good luck. But I didn't know there were scouts as early as freshman year.

"I already had one foot out the door." Dante shrugs. "It wasn't like I was ever going to play pro ball. My dad was counting down the days until I could shadow him full-time. But Christos was a hard guy not to like." He chuckles. "I actually remember the first time I noticed him. It was some team party after a loss, which was always weird. I'd just crushed two defensive linemen at beer pong when I stumbled back into the living room and found him toe-to-toe with the QB, just screaming at each other. I figured out Christos had just saved our kicker, another freshman, from a nonconsensual keg stand the quarterback lined up to 'put a little hair on his chest.' I just wanted everybody to stop fucking yelling, so I stepped in the middle and said I'd do the stand." He smiles softly. "Christos shoved me back, told me he could fight his own battles, and set the keg stand record for the year. The kicker never got shit again."

I blink furiously. I'm not tearing up. I'm not picturing the easy smile on his face in the photograph I stole, the way he used to do that when he caught Mama and Baba dancing in the kitchen. I'm the ice queen. It's a frat boy story, anyway.

"Then what?" I demand.

Dante shakes his head. "Then I graduated. I didn't see him until I managed to wriggle out of work for the homecoming game, and I could tell right away, something was different. I asked around and figured out he'd gotten tired of never having enough money for shit, so he started running drugs for the Lombardis."

I clench my jaw so he can't see my reactions. Christos never breathed a word of that. Every time he came home from school, it was all glowing recounting how cool his team was, how much everyone loved him. I assumed he was king of the school.

"Didn't take long from there." Dante frowned. "Never does. I learned this across a string of scattered games I managed to sneak off to, so I couldn't exactly do anything, but long story short, he got jumped while carrying product one night. Lost...nobody knew the exact number, but I heard somewhere between ten and a hundred thousand dollars."

"No," I whisper.

Dante raises an eyebrow at me. I lean back, try to reclaim my poise. I don't care.

"Yeah, I tried to get him out, but I was already too late. That kind of debt to a mob boss can either be paid in blood, or sweat. Christos chose sweat." He stares at his desk for a long moment. "One day, he had scouts climbing over themselves to knock on his door. The next, he'd dropped out and become a Lombardi soldier. I'm not sure he really had a choice, Eleni."

After he dropped out of school, Christos spent weeks job-hunting across the city, pounding the pavement like Baba told him to. He always came home tired, sometimes irritated, and on a few notable occasions, reeking of alcohol. I chalked all that up to the stress of finding work. Could it really have been signs of his involvement with the Lombardis?

"I didn't see him for a year." He crosses his arms. "Frank Lombardi murdered my dad. I started raiding Lombardi spots as often as I could. And one day, I turned a corner in a warehouse during the tail end of a raid to find Christos staring back at me in Lombardi colors." He meets my gaze. "He drew first, but I wasn't just going to stand there with a gun pointed at me. I tried to talk him down. Told him we could still be friends, that it didn't have to be this way. That I could get him back to his fucking parents."

He shifts his weight in the chair, his brow pinched and eyes darkening as I watch the memory of the night play over his face. He continues somberly, "he told me he wanted to be a capo. He wanted to rise through the ranks, have something to show for his life. And bagging a boss, even a baby one like me, was his ticket to the top."

Ticket to the top. That sounds like Christos. On the good days of "job-hunting," he would lay on the bed across the room from mine and tell me about what he saw for his future. His work changed every time. That was part of the game. But no matter what he did, he was the best, the brightest, an innovator like the world had never seen before. And Mama and Baba were proud. Tears sting my eyes.

"We both shot. He missed." Dante leans back in his chair like a weight has been lifted off him.

Confusion, grief, and rage swirl within me. Dante doesn't get to feel relieved after this. Christos should've known better. I should've seen the signs. Silent tears sheet down my face, the first I've cried in weeks. I stand, not sure where I'm going. Maybe Greece. Maybe the Narrows. Maybe nowhere at all.

"I caught him before he fell." Dante stands with me, holding my attention. "He had one breath to say something, and he told me not to tell his family what happened. The last thing he wanted on this Earth was for you to believe he was who he said he was. That's why I didn't tell you, El."

FALLOUT

Eleni

I gape at Dante. Christos asked him not to tell us? Why wouldn't he want us to know he was dead?

"Why should I believe you?" I say, clinging to the last vestiges of the shell I've built up.

He drops back into his seat. "That's your question to answer. I've told you everything I know. I was just keeping a promise."

My anger burns away my grief. "Keeping a promise? You lied to me, Dante. You let me—sleep with you, and you hid this from me."

"I took his body out with the rest of our men," he says like I didn't speak. "Tony and I buried him upstate. I buried him, my *friend*, with my own fucking hands. I can show you, if you want."

I slam my hands down on his desk. "Are you listening to me? What the hell made you think that would help? I'm leaving in the fucking morning."

"That's your choice," he says evenly. "But you should know this isn't a life people just get to walk away from."

"Is that a threat?"

He meets my gaze. "It's a promise. You have a reputation after these last two weeks. That brings respect, loyalty, but it also carries a price. I can't even imagine what your head is going for these days."

I scowl at him. "Oh, it's not a threat, it's a promise someone else is going to threaten me. *Real* nice."

"Listen to me, Eleni," he says quietly. "You can leave New York. My plane will be ready in the morning, but if you do, never come back."

I take a step back from the danger in his voice. "Now that's a fucking threat."

"No, I—" He shakes his head, and the aura of power radiating from him cracks. When he looks up at me again, something real shines in his dark eyes. "I love you, El, and I'm never going to stop. I don't know how I could share a city with you if we weren't—" His voice cracks. "I'd want to make you mine. Forever."

"Then let me make it easy on you." I open the door to his office and storm up the stairs to the office where I left my suitcase. It's already nearly two am. It's not like I'm going to sleep at this point. I may as well just sit at my desk, even with the crappy chair I haven't replaced.

But once I slam the door behind me, my anger starts to fizzle out, and everything seems much more complicated. Upstate. Does he mean at that safe house? Had I been that close to Christos, for the first time in years? The thought of seeing his grave summons more of the tears I'm trying to ignore. I swipe them away and circle around to sit at my desk.

There, on the top, sits my open suitcase, with the picture of Dante and Christos smiling up at me. I lift it, expecting more memories of Christos from that last summer to pour through me, but I find myself looking at Dante, thinking about what Tony said. In college, he was the life of the party. The king of the campus, like I thought Christos was. He looks like it here. There are fewer lines around his eyes, less of the fine silver threads I found in his hair. His smile is light and bright like I've seen only a few times, and it reaches his eyes easily.

I sit in the chair, picture still in hand. It would be so much easier to pack my bags and walk off into the night. But I just...can't. That last look he gave me, the way his voice cracked. Dante loves me. And, God almighty, I love him. I drop my head onto the desk. I'm so stupid.

I don't know how long I sit there for, but eventually, I realize I'm going to lose my mind if I don't do something. I hop to my feet and stride out of my room. At first, I don't know where I'm going. Or at least, I pretend I don't, until I see the pool of golden light flowing from Dante's room. My feet turn in that direction even before I've given the order. I stuff the picture into my back pocket and push the door further open.

Dante sits up in his bed wearing only a T-shirt and boxers with his eyes closed. My breath catches. Wanting him, at least, isn't stupid. He's beautiful.

"It's dangerous to sleep after a concussion," I say.

He opens one eye. "We did the whole test. I'm not concussed. And I wasn't sleeping, anyway."

His boxes sit on the floor, still unpacked. He hasn't turned the pictures around yet. My mouth goes dry. Only a few days ago, I didn't know whether Dante was going to survive. Packing him away felt right. Building a wall around my heart felt like the right course of action. Walling myself off from ever believing a word out his mouth again felt… Horrible, but here I am.

But I do believe him. His retelling of Christos' last year on this planet makes perfect sense. It's like I finally have the pieces to a puzzle I've been searching for, and that crushing burden I've been carrying on my shoulders since his disappearance lifts, leaving me feeling whole for the first time in years.

I don't recognize this feeling. This *relief*. Because that's what this is, and what he just offered me by telling me the truth.

Against all my better instincts, I climb into bed with him and rest my head in his lap. He's so warm, and when he drapes his arm wordlessly over my shoulders, the last of the ice around my heart evaporates.

I sob. Fully body, shoulders shaking, no chance of looking pretty weeping. And he just strokes his thumb back and forth over my bare upper arm in time with his heartbeat. I almost lost him. His confession felt like losing Christos all over again. I don't even know how many people I've killed. I've found something I'm really good at and it's turning me into a monster. In two weeks, my whole life has turned upside down.

When my tears start to slow, I twist and look up at him. "What were you thinking?"

"When?" he asks softly.

"When you got shot," I murmur. "When you almost left me alone here."

"El...." He gathers me up onto his chest with a wince. "Do you still love me?"

That's easy. "Of course I do. I couldn't stop if I wanted to, and trust me, I tried."

He smiles wryly. "Then I'll ask the real question. Do you still trust me?"

My heart skips a beat. I stare into his pitch-black eyes, searching for an answer I'm not sure I have yet. Whatever I say here will define the rest of my life. Do I go to Greece with Mama, or do I chase what I've found here? He strokes a few curls back from my temple with the gentlest fingers, and I know my answer.

"Yes."

Dante kisses me, and for a moment, it's like the last two weeks have disappeared. His mouth moves over mine with the same expert precision, teasing little sighs and shivers out of me. But, too fast, he leans back against the pillows, panting.

"Are you staying then?" he asks.

I bite my lip as want curls in my gut. Maybe the last two weeks don't have to disappear. Maybe we can find a new equilibrium. I nod and lean in to kiss him gently.

13

EQUILIBRIUM

Eleni

DANTE SURGES up to meet my mouth, and within moments, he has to drop back against the pillows to catch his breath again.

"I'm sorry, pet." He runs his hands up my sides. "I don't quite have my stamina back."

The siren song of old patterns calls, but I'm not the Eleni I was the last time he used that name for me. It still sends a shiver down my spine, but if we're finding a new balance, maybe we don't have to let habits dictate what comes next.

"That's okay." I nip at his earlobe, kiss down to the hollow of his throat. "I have enough stamina for the both of us."

He quirks an eyebrow at me when I lean back. I know what he's looking for. I stay silent.

"Sir?" he prompts.

"Sir just wiped out like a cartoon character walking in the front door." I smile. "So why don't you let me take the reins tonight?"

Indecision flickers across Dante's face, and for a moment, I wonder if he's ever had sex where he wasn't in charge.

Then, he says, "Okay."

Part of me didn't expect that. My breath catches, and I sit back. He really does trust me

"Tell me your colors," I say to buy a second to regain my own equilibrium.

"Green is good, yellow means I need a second, red means stop." He smirks. "Mistress."

Somehow, staring into his dark eyes, I don't find that particularly funny. It feels like slipping into a role I've been dancing around, one where I not only get to take charge but get to take care of those around me. Is this how Dante feels all the time?

I push the thought aside and return my mouth to his neck, taking my time, tasting the salt of his sweat and the scrape of his stubble. He groans and winds a hand into my hair. If the roles were reversed, he would take my hand away, but I want to feel him. He's alive, and safe, and he didn't kill Christos in cold blood. He didn't want to hurt him at all. So I drag my teeth over his tender skin and enjoy the vibrations of the resulting noise.

Before long, I reach the neck of his T-shirt. I ghost my hands down his sides to grab the hem, and he sits abruptly up.

I release his shirt. "Sit back. I'll tell you when to move. We don't need you popping more stitches."

"I'm not—"

I raise an eyebrow at him and push him back against the pillow with a single finger. He swallows and moves easily. Good. Tonight, I know what he needs. It's my job to keep him safe. That thought burns like a sip of scotch down into the fire in my gut, and I slide down his body until my face is at waist level. His cock already stands proud in his underwear, but I ignore it in favor of lifting the hem of his T-shirt a single inch and putting my mouth there. He groans, grabs my hair again, and his hips jerk, but he doesn't try to sit up. I cover the line of skin in attention, and when he doesn't do anything to hurt himself, I lift the shirt a little higher and begin again.

Working my way up his chest takes a long time, even avoiding the railway map of stitches covering half of him. I'm always careful not to put my weight on him, taking as long as I need to reposition so he's comfortable. I linger on his nipple, circling it with my tongue until the low groans falling from his lips turn into curses and his cock grows desperately hard against my waist. When I reach his defined collarbone, I lean back.

"Sit forward. Arms up."

He's panting again, but less like he needs more air and more like he's hungry. Still, he doesn't move until I give the order. I lift his shirt over his head and toss it to the side. Then, I climb off the bed. His mouth falls open in mute disappointment, and I smile.

"You hurt your hands tonight, didn't you?"

He nods.

"I don't want you to hurt anymore." I pull my shirt off, then unfasten my shorts.

Dante groans and reaches for me.

"Not ever again." The words hum through me, a promise I intend to keep far outside of this room. It's easy to strip off my bra and panties with his desperate gaze on me. Before I climb back into bed, I ease his boxers over his cock and off. The sheen of precum on the tip makes me lick my lips.

I get on the bed and straddle him, then rub my pussy back and forth over his naked cock in time with the rise and fall of his chest. God, he feels incredible. Someday soon, I'll have enough spare time to get on the pill. However people do that. For now, I ignore the voice between my legs begging me to fuck him just like this and reach for the drawer I know holds his condoms.

It takes a few seconds of blind grabbing, but I find one outside the box and tear it open with my teeth. Dante whines and runs his hands over my thighs, thrusting back up softly like he misses the friction. I burn the moment into my brain. The boss of the Staten Island Saints, wordlessly begging for me to fuck him. He trusts me too much to even ask out loud. I kiss his cheek and slide the condom on slowly. He groans again.

"Don't rush," I murmur against the shell of his ear. Then, I sink onto him.

The feeling of being full after so long pulls a groan from my lips that I don't bother hiding. Dante just stares up at me, his eyes blown wide, like every thought in his head is dedicated to not rushing, to listening. I grab his left hand, the one with fewer scrapes, and put it on one of my breasts.

He circles my nipple in time with the gentle pace I set riding him. His cock presses against my inner walls, another reason to do away with caution, but I really don't want to hurt him. I can imagine almost nothing worse than having him hand all this power to me and misusing it. So I rock against him to the beat of a heart that almost stopped, wringing moans and curses and half-shaped versions of my name from his lips. He watches me with wonder in his eyes.

"I'm close," he pants before long. "I'm sorry."

"No sorries." I brush a kiss over his lips. "I want you to feel good."

He nods. "So good."

I guide his other hand up to my hair and stay bent over him, still not putting pressure on his chest. "Then come for me."

Dante slams his hips up into mine and goes still, my name frozen on his lips. The ease with which he obeys sends me tumbling over the edge in a staggering blast of pleasure. When the aftershocks stop, I roll off him.

Not all the time. But that could be part of a new equilibrium.

14

THE CITY THAT NEVER SLEEPS

Eleni

I ROLL OVER, feeling rested for the first time in I don't even know how long, and reach for Dante. My fingers meet sheets where I know he fell asleep after our third round last night. Cold sheets. My heart leaps into my throat. I open my eyes and sit up.

Rumpled blankets. Clothes scattered everywhere. No sign of Dante. I scramble for my phone to see if Gianna or Tony has been trying to reach me with something important. A few notifications await me. One from my email, alerting me I have an unsaved draft. I swipe that away. I tried to write a polite "no, thank you" back to Professor Calhoun yesterday, and it's the last thing I need to think about right now. A few general check-ins and junk. One from Gianna that I open without reading the message preview.

Hello?? Tell me you didn't literally leave for Greece without texting me goodbye.

I blink. Then, my gaze drifts to the time she sent the message. Eleven am. My heart skips another beat, and I check the time now. Nearly noon.

61

"Shit!" I don't think I've ever slept this late in my life, between school and the restaurant. I've missed half the day already. I snag Dante's crumpled T-shirt off the end of the bed and slide it on over my naked body. I can't remember what day of the week it is, but there's nearly always some house staff around, so I need something to wear down the hall to get dressed.

My feet slide on the wooden floor when I leap out of bed and tear for the door. I don't even know if Dante told all the men he's back in charge yet, or if he really is after last night. I certainly received a few check-ins from soldiers. I fling open the door and sprint down the hall toward my room.

Someone clears their throat. I skid to a halt. There, in the foyer where they can clearly see me, stand three Staten Island Saints. Seb and two other soldiers whose names I haven't learned yet. My face burns, but I straighten up like I'm wearing one of my suits.

"Morning," I say sharply.

"Morning." Seb smirks. "Late night?"

I flip him the bird and stomp to my room. No point in pretending. Just to spite them, despite the summer heat, I change into a turtleneck and jeans before heading downstairs.

Seb is still snickering when I reach the bottom.

"I see you made up," he says. "Or should I be ducking for cover before a mostly naked bartender flees the scene?"

I punch him in the arm. "I thought I was the boss around here."

Seb quirks an eyebrow as he starts to walk down the hall toward Dante's office. "I thought the boss was back, and you got demoted." He smirks again. "*Dee*-moted, if you know what I mean."

I roll my eyes. "Real mature. We're, uh, still figuring that out." I think. At least telling Seb probably won't cause too much trouble.

He nods. "Badass. I guess you do have a few capo-level kills under your belt."

"And then some." My mind wanders to what Dante said last night about making a name for myself. We reach the door to his office and find it closed. "Do you know what's going on in there?"

Seb blows out a breath through his teeth. "Nothing good, as far as I can tell."

"Great." I reach for the doorknob. "I'll go get my own answers."

"Hey!" Seb grabs my wrist. "Why don't we…uh…yeah, this isn't gonna work. Dante asked me to keep you out here because you've got other shit to do today."

I frown. "No, I don't. And if he thinks he can talk a good game when no one's looking and then box me out as soon as the sun comes up, he's got another thing coming."

Before I can reach for the door again, Dante, Tony, and a handful of capos including Armando pour out. Armando shoots me an apologetic shrug.

"All right, everyone go make sure your soldiers are on the same page," Dante says.

The capos start to walk away, but Tony remains.

"Except me, right?"

Dante nods. "Take Seb if you think you need back-up. Get it done."

I stare at the man who whined for my touch last night as Tony grabs Seb and marches out in my peripheral vision.

"What the hell is happening? I haven't even had coffee yet."

"I'll start that." Dante wraps an arm around my waist and kisses my cheek. "Go get dressed. I left a new outfit for you in my closet. We have a few errands to run today."

"Errands?" I blink. "Why was everyone—?"

He smiles indulgently. "If I tell you a little, will you go? We don't want to be late."

I nod, only half-sure I actually woke up.

"It's Cal Duncan," he says. "Nothing bad. He's just throwing a little money around where he doesn't belong."

My synapses take a few seconds to connect the dots, but finally, I get there. Cal Duncan, boss of the Irish Kings, motherfucker in the city I had pegged as most likely to cause trouble soon.

Dante must see the recognition dawn, because he pats my butt and says, "Now get going."

Blearily, I obey. Everything is happening so fast. But I go to the closet he described and find a garment bag emblazoned with a designer label. Inside sits a cobalt blue skirt-suit, a white shirt to go underneath, and a pair of matching, red-bottomed heels. It looks like something I'd pick out over the last few weeks, with a bit more color. And of course, when I put it on, it fits perfectly. I admire myself in the mirror for a moment, pull my hair up in a quick bun like Gianna taught me, and add a little bit of lip gloss and mascara. My uniform in Dante's absence. Then, my head still spinning, I trudge downstairs with the heels in hand.

Dante waits for me at the bottom with a steaming to-go cup of coffee in hand. I didn't even know we had those. I snatch the beverage out of his hands and sip greedily.

Two creams, two sugars. Just like I used to take it. Which he doesn't know changed. I pull the cup away from my lips and eye him.

"What exactly are we doing today?"

He just smiles and offers me his arm.

15

SINCE YOU'RE STAYING

Dante

I PULL the car up in front of the abstract red sculpture that marks the front of the Tandon Institute, and Eleni turns to me with a glare.

"What the hell are we doing here?"

I park. "You know, I think the sculpture looks like a bunch of checkers falling over. What about you?"

"Dante." She crosses her arms. "Answer me."

I smile. I knew she was going to react like this. In truth, I don't really care. She's staying. She's finding a way to get used to the fact that I killed Christos. It's not over between us, and I don't have to spend the rest of my life wishing I never told her. Even the ache in my chest can't bring me down today. I climb out of the car without answering, circle around the hood, and try to open her door.

It's locked. She locked it. She stares through the window at me, arms still crossed.

"Answers, or I'm not getting out," she calls through the bulletproof glass.

I exhale heavily. How has she gotten more stubborn? I was only gone for two weeks.

"Is 'you're going to be late in five minutes' enough?"

"Late for what?" she replies.

"Registration." I can't help the smile that creeps over my lips.

Her mouth falls open. "Registration? Here? Dante, why are you doing this?"

I smooth a hand over my hair and thank whoever's listening that the campus is quiet on this midsummer day. Without students streaming into and out of the glass building behind me, I'm just another man negotiating with a car in New York City. No one's even going to look twice.

"I glanced over your books," I admit. I woke up earlier than any doctor would be happy to hear, and I needed something to do this morning. "It all seemed like jargon, so I took a look at your notes. God, El, I didn't understand a fucking word, but I can tell you're smart."

She bites her lips and flicks her gaze to the building behind me. My heart leaps. She's listening. And she looks like a fucking dream.

"And...I saw that email." I smile sheepishly like I didn't go looking to see if she'd said anything back. "You had half an apology typed up. Something about appreciating his faith in you, wishing you could accept, but you had to...." I lean against the car. "You don't have to go anywhere anymore. Since you're staying, you should take advantage of this opportunity."

She fiddles with the lock. "Do you have any idea how much a semester at Tandon costs?"

"$31,123," I say blithely. "Which I already have earmarked for this upcoming semester."

She stares at me for a long moment. One long, dark curl has tumbled out of her bun to frame her face, and I just want to pull on it. She deserves this. And a million other things. I just need her to let me provide.

"I can't go full-time," she says as she opens the car door. "And I doubt I can live on campus. I live in Staten Island now–"

"Why not?" I loop my arm through hers and start leading her into the building before she can run.

She raises an eyebrow. "I'm still a Saint. And you were the one who was all over me last night about how much danger I've put myself in, these last two weeks. Don't you remember what happened when I tried to take my last final?"

I frown as we board the elevator. Seb and her guards got kidnapped by Luca Lombardi's people, but that's not normal. Hell, I went to college and survived.

"All of my capos have jobs outside of the syndicate," I say. "Tony runs a carwash. Did he ever tell you that?"

"He did." Eleni drops her voice to a whisper as we exit the elevator on the third floor. "Right before he told me that was how I should clean the money we cleaned out of that warehouse in Jersey."

"A job's a job." I wave my hand airily. "Go talk to the registrar. See what they have, what excites you. We can talk logistics later."

"But—"

I open the door the nice assistant gave me directions to on the phone this morning, grab Eleni by the shoulders, and shove her in. Up here, a few students mill back and forth, and I stand out too like a sore thumb in my suit. During that call, the assistant told me the meeting would take anywhere from half an hour to an hour, so I wander until I find a cluster of chairs and sit.

Try to sit. I slide on the egg-shaped orange leather for a few seconds before giving up, leaning on one of the floor to ceiling windows, and pull out my phone. It hasn't been that long since I was in college, but the air here feels completely different than it did at Wagner. Maybe it's the difference in majors. Maybe it's just how much staggeringly smarter the people here are than the ones there. We had some eggheads, but Tandon produces Nobel Prize winners. There's no contest.

Everything Tony told me about El running the Saints plays through my mind, and for the first time, I wonder if she's not wasting her time in the mafia. Not for any protective reasons—though I'd still kill to get her out, let her live on campus, just have a normal college experience—but because her talents are wasted with us. That sends a frisson of nerves up my spine, and I pull out my phone to call Tony.

"How's it going?" he says, his voice layered with innuendo.

"Fuck off," I reply. "We're at the registrar."

Tony chuckles. "I think people usually wait longer to get cold feet."

A couple of students burst into laughter, and I tuck my phone closer to my ear, as if they could hear me.

"My feet are nice and fucking toasty. I have to do this."

He sighs. "Are you doing this to protect her, or because you want to?"

I bristle. "Because she's staying, she needs protection. Of course."

"Right." Tony lets the biting sarcasm linger for a moment. "Just calling to chat? Should I get one of those phone cords to wind around my finger while we giggle about crushes?"

He might be my best friend, but sometimes, Tony is the worst fucking person to talk to about shit. I grit my teeth and stare out over the street, the hum of New York City that Eleni will be embedded within when she comes here. It's better than Staten Island for her. I know that. I have to keep her in the real world as much as I can. I can't lose that part of her yet.

"Have you gotten me that face-to-face with Cal yet?" I ask.

"Working on it," Tony replies. "If you've got a free evening, he might be—"

My phone vibrates. I pull it away from my head to check. A text from Eleni, wondering where I am. She's already out. I don't know whether that's a good sign or bad.

"Set it up," I tell Tony. "I have to go."

I hang up before he can make another joke and hurry back through the halls. When I find Eleni, she's standing outside the office, her face slightly pink and a new-student folder clutched in both hands.

"How much did you donate? They said I didn't even have to worry about the application process," she demands.

I tuck my arm through hers and smile. "Where do you want to go to lunch?"

She doesn't need to know how little it was after Professor Calhoun's glowing recommendation, and how much more I'd pay to see that little blush again.

16

—————

PRETTY WOMAN

Eleni

WHEN I JOKED that we should go shopping before lunch, have the whole commuter experience, I didn't expect Dante to take me up on it. I certainly didn't expect him to trail after me through designer store after designer store, making introductions to the right clerks and offering opinions on my choices. I look at the two extra chairs they had to pull over to our table in the ridiculously upscale if tiny French bistro, both piled with bags full of purchases. I have no idea what's going on. All I know is there's a real chance we just spent as much as the semester at Tandon, even with the ridiculous bribe he probably had to make, and he's still smiling at me over the most expensive burger I've ever heard of.

At the very least, spending his money feels great. It was the one thing I was scared to do with him gone, and after his behavior at the warehouse the other day, he deserves it.

I deserve a little treat from time to time, and based on the look on his face, he likes doing this. He likes taking care of me.

71

I need to get used to that if I'm staying. But we've never had a day like this to ourselves. There's always been an ulterior motive.

"What are we doing?" I ask.

"Errands." He pops the last bite of burger into his mouth.

Errands. Right. Because errands always include a burger with a truffle-foie gras sauce and the croque madame in front of me. Honestly, I keep expecting to start chasing down Cal Duncan, or run into him in one of these upscale shops. He checks his phone just often enough that I know there's something going down. I just don't quite know what, and I'm getting tired of that very quickly.

"What's your favorite purchase so far?" he asks.

I look over the bags. There are at least a dozen new suits in there, including a purchase slip from his personal tailor who "wouldn't dream" of letting us walk out with something he hadn't perfectly fitted. But Dante also insisted on checking off the new-student purchase list in the folder the very officious registrar pushed on me in the thunderstorm of information, so I reach for one very square bag that barely fits its contents.

"The laptop, for sure."

"Yeah?" Dante looks over the box. "How's, uh…how's it different from your current one?"

I sigh. During these last two weeks, I realized Dante looks like a modern mafia boss with all his technology in place, but his cyberse-curity was worse than Baba insisted on for the restaurant. He didn't even own an external hard drive before I bought one and spent a day copying all the important files onto there before storing it in a safe. And that doesn't even factor the time I spent installing any firewalls to keep some kid fifteen minutes out of Quantico from cracking open his operation like a steamed clam.

"Better RAM," I say. "I can download my own OS, and it has enough ports for all the supplementary drives I expect to need to plug in."

Dante blinks. "Right. And OS is…?"

"Operating system." I smile. "But don't worry, grandpa, there won't be a quiz at the end of lunch."

He fakes hurt. "Grandpa? I'll have you know my phone has several applications *and* a game."

I meet his gaze. "What game?"

His dramatic expression falls into something more serious. "Okay, it's solitaire, but the other ones are too busy!"

I laugh so hard I almost get gruyere on my new shirt, barely believing how far I've come from the Eleni I was a few months ago, pirating my textbooks and struggling to get homework done between shifts. When my laughter finally tapers off, I look up to find him on his phone again.

My humor dies. Right. We can never forget about work. I huff and sit back up.

He glances at me. "What's wrong?"

I push the laptop back into the bag and gesture at the chairs full of stuff. "Why are you buttering me up? Is there bad news coming?"

"No." He looks at his phone like he barely heard me. "Are you ready to go?"

I look at my half-finished sandwich, his untouched fries. More shopping can't hurt, I guess. Though the longer this goes on, the meaner it feels that I haven't made him stop.

When I nod, he signals the waiter for the check, then presses a couple hundred-dollar bills into the teenager's hand without even looking.

"Care to drop this all in the car?" he asks when we're outside.

"Will you tell me where we're going next?" I ask.

"Aurora's." He grins at me.

Another brand I've never heard of. It doesn't sound like somewhere I'd find a brutally violent Irish man. I sigh and agree.

We pile armfuls of bags into the car, then Dante leads me down a few streets and over one. I study the storefronts. This road is a little less polished than most of the others we've been on today, with smaller, darker buildings that obviously sit under huge towers of apartments. A little old lady nods to Dante as we pass, and I frown.

"Where are we?" I ask.

"One of the many Italian parts of this town." He smiles. "Walk tall.

I wasn't planning on making introductions today, but a good first impression never hurts."

I straighten. Work, always work. We're not just Eleni and Dante, we're the king and queen of the Staten Island Saints.

That is, I think we are. He hasn't said anything about me continuing to be involved like I was yet. And he seems to be trying to get me to leave Staten Island all together. Even if I can manage full-time school on top of mafia work, I definitely can't do it while living on campus. I can't share a bedroom with some eighteen-year-old and have to worry about her finding the guns I never go anywhere without anymore.

Dante stops in front of one small store. I can just barely make out the word "Aurora's" in faded gold paint over the door. He opens the door, a bell jingles, and he gestures me inside. I stride into the dark shop.

Immediately, I realize it's dark inside because the proprietor only lit the glass cases full of glittering jewelry. In the dim store, they shine like stars, drawing my eye instantly. I drift over to the nearest one and stare, open-mouthed, at some of the most beautiful necklaces I've ever seen in my life. I put a hand to my neck and remember I'm still not wearing the tracker.

"'Ey!" someone barks.

I jump back. Dante appears behind me, solid but unstartled. One of the tiniest old men I've ever seen bustles out from behind a beaded curtain and hops up on a stool behind the counter.

"Dino?" he says.

I glance at Dante. Unlike when his uncle used the old name, Dante grins.

"Louie!" He spreads his arms. "Been too long."

Louie spits below the counter. "Never long enough. Thought I told you not to darken my door again."

"You say that every time." Dante approaches the counter. "And I fear for the day you mean it."

Louie sniffs. I study the old man, but despite his gruff demeanor, there's no aggression in his face or his stance. That might just be how he greets people.

"We're looking for a ring size." Dante nods at me. "For this one."

Louie looks me up and down. "Queen of Saints, huh? Was wondering when you'd finally deign to cross the bridge."

"Sorry," I say. "I would've come if I'd known. Your work is beautiful."

"I know that." He pulls something out from under the counter. "Hand?"

I offer my left hand out of instinct and look at Dante. "Should I be bracing for you to get down on one knee?"

Louie slides a metal circle, like a plain ring, onto my index finger.

He laughs. "Just looking for another way to put a tracker on you. I said rings work better."

Joking with Dante feels like going back to normal, but I can't ignore how unsettled things remain between us.

"Then we should measure you too," I say as Lousie trades the circle out for another one, then moves onto the next finger.

Dante raises an eyebrow.

"I said I'd wear a tracker if you did." I wish Louie was done so I could cross my arms. "It's time to pay up."

Dante glances at Louie, who lifts another collection of metal circles from behind the counter.

"I have men's sizers," he says. "And I'll do anything to get you two out of here."

Dante looks from the sizers to me and back again. "Will this really make you more comfortable?"

"To know that you keep your promises? Yes."

Dante sighs and sets his hand on the counter. "Me next, Lou."

"Louie," the old man barks.

I meet Dante's gaze, and something like I felt in bed last night courses through me. I'm no longer the little virgin he bought at the auction who'd do anything he asked. I'm enough of a force that he has to listen to me. But underneath that is something else. Something I haven't felt in a really long time.

Hope.

17

NIGHT ON THE TOWN

Eleni

WE WALK OUT of Louie's shop, and I blink in the summer sun. Everything that happened in the tiny jewelry shop starts to feel like a dream.

"What now?" I ask. "Can we finally go home and deal with whatever makes you keep checking your phone?"

Abruptly, I realize he hasn't looked at his phone since we stepped into Aurora's. But I'd be surprised if Louie had ever heard of Wi-Fi, much less spent his mornings texting prospective clients.

"Yes and no." Dante smiles. "I'm done with my phone, because everything is arranged, but we're not going home."

I scowl at him. My feet are starting to hurt. Maybe I need to build up stamina before I invite Gianna on one of these. I've watched a few of her shows now, and it seems like stamina is the one thing a pole dancer needs in spades.

"We are going to stay the night in the city at a five-star hotel," Dante says.

A SHORT WALK, a conversation with a very snooty concierge, and a strangely tense elevator ride later, I stride into a suite near the top floor of a hotel I've passed for my whole life and never once imagined being allowed inside. It's beyond my wildest dreams.

The front room has the same white marble floor as the lobby Dante basically floated through, and aside from a long table for keys and a coat closet, the only thing in the room is a massive grand piano with a chandelier dangling over top. My breath catches. I've never even stayed in a hotel that had a front room. One really good year, Mama and Baba took us on a trip to the Jersey shore, and we stayed in this tiny little hotel right next to the beach. They shared the bed, and Christos and I shared the pull-out couch next to it. Back then, I'd thought just going on a vacation was the height of luxury.

Dante marches through the door, tossed his tie on the piano bench, and keeps going.

"Shower, or bath?"

"What?" I blink, instinctively pinching my forearm to confirm this is a dream.

"Do you want to take a shower, or a bath?"

"Shower? But, um, why do I need either? It's still basically afternoon."

"Just to freshen up." He smiles. "I had some clothes sent ahead for me, but yours should be arriving shortly."

Clothes. Multiple bathrooms. I drift after Dante for lack of anything better to do. I feel like I've stepped into another world entirely and I barely know up from down, let alone what he has in store for me while we're here. The white marble front room gives way to a deep blue kitchen that almost rivals the one in Dante's house for size. After that is a huge living room with couches the same blue as the kitchen. On either side of a wall of floor-length windows stand two doors.

He can't really live like this. Nobody can. When I follow him into the bedroom, he already has his shirt off, revealing the tanned expanse of his chest. Before I can say anything, a gong rings through the space.

"Doorbell." He smiles apologetically and darts away.

I look around the master bedroom—the bed is bigger than mine, Christos', and Mama and Baba's put together—and find a garment bag hanging in the closet. I unzip it slowly. Inside sits a pure black tuxedo with a dove-gray shirt and an emerald bow tie. I don't know whether the gray or the color surprises me more. But Dante returns before I can decide with yet another garment bag in hand. My head is spinning faster than it was at Tandon.

"We're running a little short on time, but let me know what you think." He unzips the bag.

My breath catches. A full-length gown the same green as the bow tie spills out. I run my finger over the billowing satin skirt and nearly cry at how soft it is. There are slits in the equally simple bodice, along the ribs, but when I investigate them, they lead back to a pair of ribbons that actually tie the top in place. Meaning I'll be trusting my breasts to my knot-tying skills and the minuscule spaghetti straps.

Oh, god, the dress is beautiful. It belongs in this suite, in this world. I fidget with the suit Dante also picked out for me and try not to feel about six inches tall.

"Wear your hair up with this," he murmurs. "I want to see your neck while I'm making dull conversation with billionaires at the Met's charity gala this evening. Thinking about sinking my teeth into it will keep me going."

I gape. A *gala*? The first reference he's made all day to us spending the night together. It's too much to process at once, especially the day after I start to step out of weeks of ice. I sit abruptly down on the bed and blink back tears.

"Hey." He hangs the dress up and sits behind me. "You also don't have to. You can stay here, if you want. I'm sorry I didn't say anything before, it was a last minute thing. I normally don't go to these things when I'm invited–"

I shake my head. "It's not you. It's just…you." I laugh wetly.

He stares at me in bemusement. "That makes it tough to help."

"It's everything you come with." I gesture around at the suite. "You're so used to this life. I feel like I'm pretending."

Dante takes my hand and meets my gaze. "Can I tell you a secret?"

I bite my lip and nod.

"I barely had to donate to NYU," he says. "They wanted you. I gave them a little donation in good faith when I said I'd be paying your tuition, that's all. You did this on your own, El."

My heart skips a beat. That can't be true. The Tandon Institute has notoriously high standards.

Like he can see the disbelief on my face, he pulls out his phone, opens a banking app, and shows me a transaction. I blink a few times, then rub my eyes. The number on the screen is smaller than a semester of tuition. It's probably smaller than what he spent on that incredible dress.

He paid to let me cut the line. He didn't pay to put me in line at all. Maybe I haven't grown up in this life, or worn dresses like that, but I whipped the Staten Island Saints into shape in two weeks and I got into the Tandon Institute after two night college classes. The old billionaires at the Met aren't going to know what hit them... But I still wonder why exactly Dante would be going to an event like this in the first place.

I guess I'll find out.

I stand, grab the dress, and hurry to the other bedroom to change. After a quick shower, I blow dry my hair and stare at the dress. The bra I picked out certainly won't work with it, and while I found a pair of glittering earrings and some sky-high heels in the bag, there wasn't any underwear. So I have to go without.

And after my tiny breakdown, I don't want Dante to forget I'm more than I used to be, so I kick all my undergarments into the corner. Another wave of emotion shivers through me as I imagine him sliding his hand under my dress during dinner, discovering the steps I skipped. Maybe Dante won't know what hit him either.

I order a few cosmetics through room service, scamper out to grab them without putting the dress on, and get to work. A quick call with Gianna results in an even more complex updo than the one I had previously and my first ever smoky eye. Then I slide the dress on over my head, zipper up the skirt, gather the ribbons in one hand, and walk into the main room with it still untied.

Dante's jaw drops when he sees me. He twists on the couch as I walk, as if he's trying to keep me in view at all times. The breeze under the skirt reminds me just how close I am to naked, an electric feeling that shoots down my spine. I saunter up to him, turn, and offer the ribbons.

"Help me out?" I ask.

"Always." Dante grabs the ribbons, and I drop my hands.

Rookie mistake. He releases the ribbons a second later and slides his hands over my bare rib cage. His fingers brush the bottoms of my breasts.

"Fuck the gala," he murmurs.

I lean back into him as pleasure courses through me. What do I care about a gala? He nips the juncture of my neck and my shoulder, then slides one hand up over my breast and the other lower. When he realizes he's not finding underwear, he groans loudly. I grin.

"No, I think I want to go out." I step away from him, and his hands slip out from under the satin. "Tie me up, please?"

He groans again. "You're right, but God, El."

I grab the ribbons and offer them to him again. After a few more complaints, he does fasten the top.

"Maybe we'll leave early," he grumbles.

"Maybe." I grin at him and walk ahead, humming.

18

KINGS AND QUEENS

Eleni

DANTE LEADS me through the lobby, his gaze barely leaving my cleavage, and out into a waiting limo. Today has been so crazy I don't even ask where the other car with our shopping went. But as we pull into traffic, I do notice the two nondescript sedans that pull out behind us. My heart picks up speed until I spot the license plates. Both Saints cars. They're nothing more than an escort. Dante is quiet on the ride to the Metropolitan Museum of Art, but I'm bouncing in my seat. I look incredible, feel incredible, and I can't wait to find out what the hell kind of gala a mafioso goes to and more importantly, why.

When the limo pulls up outside, I have to smother a laugh. A massive banner dangling over the front of the stone edifice declares a benefit for a charity helping misguided and underprivileged youth.

"Who are you, Dante?"

"What?" Dante smiles as he opens the door. "You don't think I have hidden depths?"

I'm about to meet a completely different side of him. Cameras

83

flash as he steps out, then holds out a hand for me. Part of me worries we shouldn't be seen. But judging by his megawatt smile, he knew exactly what we were walking into, and he wouldn't put me in danger unnecessarily. I take his hand and step out.

I think I get it, at least, I'm starting to understand how the dark, underground mafia world operates. Dante has an insane amount of money, that's clear, but he can let it rot away somewhere unseen. I wonder if going to these events and throwing his money at these charities is just another way for him to clean his money, to throw the feds off his trail.

More cameras flash as we walk up the stairs. It's not as dramatic as I feared from the inside of the limo, just a handful of photographers and nobody asks us any questions, but it's far closer to the red-carpet treatment than I've ever received before. Dante doesn't let go of my hand as we enter the museum itself and follow a few signs to a European sculpture court. I haven't been to the Met since high school, and the building feels so much bigger than it did when I was wandering it with a notepad, trying to come up with essay topics.

In the sculpture court, long tables thread between the statues, and people mill in errant spirals, clutching flutes of champagne and tiny hors d'oeuvres. Before I can even think to ask, a waiter in black appears next to us.

"Mr. Cattaneo." The young man smiles. "I can get you your usual scotch. Champagne for your lovely date?"

He looks at me. I've never had champagne before. I nod.

The waiter hands me a flute and a small napkin. "My name is Enrico, please find me if you need a refill."

I nod, and Dante leads me deeper into the event.

"They know you here?" I whisper over the quiet classical music emanating from somewhere.

"Certainly." Dante waves at someone across the room. "I'm a soft-hearted billionaire. I come by a few times a year, donate aggressively and tip even more so."

I start to smile up at him, then pale. "Should I have tipped Enrico?"

He chuckles. "Enrico and I have an arrangement. I give him a few dollars throughout, and then he finds me at the end for his real tip so his catering company doesn't take a percentage."

I nod. "Okay, and—"

An older black man emerges out of the crowd with a gorgeous woman in a glittering red dress at his side. "Cat! I thought we were going to miss you this time around."

"Mr. Washington." Dante shakes his hand warmly. "And Mrs. Washington, my god, you look incredible."

The woman on the man's arm smiles prettily, highlighting the smile lines carved into her dark skin. "You are a charmer. You have to be careful, Andre, or Cat's going to steal me away."

Andre laughs. "After the bill for this last dress, you can have her. But for the first time, I notice there's no room on your arm."

My heart leaps into my throat. I'm not just a bystander watching this. "Hi, I'm—"

"Eleni Calimeris," Dante says smoothly. "My girlfriend. I'm sorry, Mrs. Washington, but you've missed your window."

She laughs. Andre laughs. Dante laughs. I force myself to laugh with them, even though my stomach is humming with butterflies. Dante called me his girlfriend! To other people!

The rest of the night passes like that. A blur of people with crisp diction that says they went to private school fawning over Dante and his various contributions until he introduces me and begins bragging about my accomplishments. I explain that I'm starting at Tandon so many times the news almost becomes mundane. Almost. Enrico plies Dante with scotch, me with champagne. I try tiny appetizers with names I can barely pronounce. Someone gets up on the stage and announces some award. My laughter comes easier and easier. So does Dante's.

"Do you want to look at the rest of the museum?" he murmurs. "Get some air?"

My face feels warm. Air would be good. I nod, and he leads me out toward more sculptures. Cool air washes over my face, and the noise fades behind us.

"Who are you, and what the hell have you done with the Dante I know?" I ask as soon as we have a little privacy.

He laughs and tucks my arm more securely through his. "Believe it or not, my investment portfolio isn't just a way to clean money."

"Underprivileged kids?" I raise an eyebrow.

He leads me past a room with a few occupants loudly talking about overseas banking. "I donate to anything that makes a difference here in the city. If it's out on Staten Island, even better." He shrugs. "I like the ego boost that comes with charity, but I like it best when I can actually see the effects in my neighborhoods. It feels like giving back a little of what I've taken."

I stare up at him and find nothing but earnest truth in his dark eyes. "Do you even collect protection money?"

He grimaces. "Not when I can help it. My father didn't have the same compunctions, and phasing out the practice is tougher than you'd think."

I nod. "So you're not exactly breaking kneecaps over it."

"Never."

Neither of us has to say the name Lombardi to summon them into the conversation. I can almost taste Baba's blood on my tongue, and I wash it down with the remainder of my champagne. It's not so bad. A little bitter, but the bubbles make me smile. Dante leads me into a gallery without another word.

Greek and Roman sculptures span the room. Together, we wander over to a full-body nude of a young man throwing a discus. I smirk.

"I guess it's good you don't take after your ancestors."

"What?" Dante asks.

I nod at the discus-thrower's junk with another sly smile, and Dante laughs.

"Oh, I see where your mind is." He pulls me over to a female nude. "Well, what do you have to say about this one?"

I circle it thoughtfully, barely holding back a torrent of laughter. "Yeah, my ass is a lot better."

He grins. "Are you sure about that?"

I glance around the empty gallery, then turn my back to him and lift my skirt. "You tell me."

"El!" I feel his warmth, the material of his tuxedo against me a second later. "Anyone could see you."

"Let them look." I turn to face him and drop my skirt. The champagne bubbled away all my insecurities. "I belong in here with the rest of the art."

Dante groans. "You've got that right. Let me—" He glances around, then starts leading me away from the statue.

When he pulls me into the corner, I realize he's found the only place in the room people won't be able to see just walking past the doors. I wrap my arms around his neck and crush my mouth to his.

Gentleness flies out of my mind. He devours me, and I meet every move with one of my own. Wetness gathers between my legs, another reminder of how little I have on. Dante runs his hand up my thigh, baring swaths of skin, and I press into him. More, I need more. His fingers ghost over my clit and—

"Cattaneo!" somebody with an accent I can't quite place calls.

Dante steps immediately back from me and fixes my skirt, all playfulness disappearing from his face. "We're not just here for a good time, El."

I blink, confused by the sudden shift. "We're not?"

"No." He takes my hand and begins striding out of the sculpture room. He squeezes my hand. "We're also here to meet Cal Duncan."

19

FACE TO FACE

Eleni

I STRUGGLE to tamp down my libido as Dante pulls me out of the sculpture gallery. Cal Duncan? Here? With all the champagne, I forgot the day started with his name. For all my research, I haven't been able to find a picture of the guy, so I have no idea who to look for in the crowd of well-dressed partygoers.

"Mr. Cattaneo." A man with deep red hair and a lilting Irish accent steps into our path. "And Ms. Calimeris. What a pleasant surprise."

Before I can reply, he takes my hand and kisses my knuckles. I blink, fighting for coherency. Instead, I notice the fine sprinkling of freckles on Cal's sharp cheekbones and the amusement in his light brown eyes. The charming man in front of me doesn't match any of the horrifying stories I heard about him.

"Mr. *Duncan.*" Dante's voice sounds strained as he sticks out his hand to shake. "I was so hoping to see you tonight."

"Is that so?" Cal releases my hand and shakes Dante's. "I heard you'd been absent from the circuit for a while. It seems to me you're the one people should be looking for, not the other way around."

Something flashes in Dante's eyes, and he doesn't release Cal's hand. "I'm afraid those rumors have been greatly exaggerated. I'm just as much a presence as always."

Cal nods slowly, and I glance at their entwined hands. Both of their knuckles have turned white with how hard they're gripping each other, all while smiling politely.

"I was making the rounds for a while," I say. "Mr. Cattaneo was a bit…gala'd out."

Cal looks at me, and his polite smile widens into something almost genuine. Or mocking.

"I'd heard this as well," he says. "The fabled Queen of Saints." He glances around. "For all your contributions, of course."

A cluster of people from the gala walk past us, laughing tipsily. Moments ago, I was one of them. Now, my heart pounds in my throat as I struggle to hold onto my tongue and my thoughts long enough to survive this run-in.

"Well, it seems fairly obvious to me," Dante says, "that I intend to remain on the circuit. The charities on this side of town no longer need your help to stay afloat, Mr. Duncan."

"Ah." Cal's smile grows tight again. "Well, as long as I get my invitation to your annual barbecue, I'm happy to make sure the money is spread out around the city. Capiche, as you would say?"

Dante stares at him for a long moment, then releases his hand. "Understood. Enjoy your evening, Mr. Duncan."

Cal bows dramatically to me, claps Dante on the shoulder, and pushes between us to stride away. Dante takes my hand and leads me in the opposite direction.

"He's not what I expected," I murmur. "What, exactly, just happened between the two of you?"

"Not all enemies are like the Lombardis," Dante replies. "Cal hasn't technically crossed the line yet. He was feeling me out as much as I was." He runs his tongue over his lower teeth.

I frown. "I know he sent men into Italian territory."

"Who—" Dante shakes his head. "Don't tell me. Keep the men you earned. Yes, he crossed territory lines, but not personally, and I knocked their teeth in. Business is the line that starts a war."

I squeeze his hands gently. "Business or personal."

Dante looks down at me, some of his bravado melting away. "Yes."

I tagged the Irish Kings last week as a potential problem. They have more men than us and a share of the city that rivals what we gained from killing Luca. And a history of making impulsive, dangerous choices.

"I've heard scary shit about the Kings," I admit. "Is it true they burned down five Russian warehouses in one night?"

Dante nods and steers me away from the crowds. "And that they locked the doors before lighting the matches. The Russians had a strict policy of helping out the widows of anyone killed on their payroll, and the Kings knew that many deaths would hamstring their cashflow."

Innocent deaths. I ordered more than my fair share of murders over the last two weeks, but never of innocents. I barely resist the urge to glance over my shoulder and make sure Cal is still walking away. He scares me almost as much as the rest of the Kings put together.

I drop my voice to a whisper. "I also heard Cal killed his own father to take over early."

Dante's grip on my hand tightens. "Nobody can confirm that except Cal himself. And it's not exactly the kind of rumor that endears people to him."

"If he's willing to do all that, why—" I blink, and clarity dawns through the lingering haze in my brain. "He wanted to see us. And you made sure it was in public, where he couldn't do anything worse than crush your hand."

"Close."

Soft classical music pours down the hall ahead, a promise we're nearly back at the main gala. Back when Cal Duncan wouldn't dare try anything.

"He didn't want to see us," Dante says. "He wanted to see you. I told him I could make that happen as long as he stayed on his side of the fence. I have business with him now that the Lombardis and Coppola territory is mine."

My stomach swoops. Maybe Dante wasn't being ridiculous about the danger. "So… He wanted to see me, and in exchange, he'd stay out of Saint Territory?"

He nods, smirking. "I don't think you realize the impression you made on the other outfits, El. You're a legend." He sighs, giving my hand a few more gentle squeezes. "But I don't want him to spoil our night." He tucks my hand through his arm. "Let's eat, dance, and get thoroughly drunk."

"One last question." I peer up at him. "What's the annual barbecue?"

Dante grins. "Exactly what it sounds like."

WE TUMBLE out of the limo in front of the hotel at nearly one in the morning, and I cling to Dante's arm, giggling. Cal left the gala after our run-in, and Enrico was very good at earning his tips, so the floaty feeling that chased me through the sculpture gallery is back in full force. If the wide, bright smile on Dante's face is anything to go by, he's not far behind.

"Careful!" He catches my waist before I can topple off my heels and pulls me flush against his body.

My heart pounds in my chest, then my stomach, then between my legs. The streetlights turn Dante's eyes into something brilliant and sparkling. I lean up and kiss him.

It's like igniting a firework. Dante's hands roam my body as he devours my mouth, his teeth in my lips and his tongue battling with mine. The city fades away around us. He cups my breasts, follows the line of the ribbon around to the back.

"We should go inside," he growls.

I don't care. I kiss him again.

"Pet." His voice is sharp with command, and I obey instantly, stepping back on the sidewalk.

Part of me rebels. What happened to the last two weeks? Haven't I spent all this time finding my place in his world? The rest of me feels so natural falling into step beside him as he walks into the hotel that I can't imagine doing anything else. My body hums with anticipation, and I decide the rules can be different in the bedroom.

Or wherever else Dante wants me.

2 0

HOW HIGH?

Dante

I STUDY Eleni in the reflection of the chrome elevator doors, nearly salivating. Her breasts are about to burst out of that dress of hers, one tug of a ribbon away from total exposure. And I know she's not wearing anything under the skirt. I nearly took her in the museum, and again on the street. It would be so easy. But after the past two weeks of everything spinning out of my control, I want to see just how good she'll be for me and only me.

The elevator doors open, and she starts to step out.

"Where are you going, pet?" I ask, low and dangerous.

She freezes. "The room?"

"Did I tell you to move?" I sweep my gaze over her body.

She shakes her head. "Sorry, sir."

I wait three heartbeats. "Let's go."

The hunger that burns through me when she follows a step behind me the whole way down the hall threatens to burn me to ash. I'm already half hard in these fucking suit pants. Tonight is going to be incredible.

95

I slide the keycard into the door and say, "From now on, you're not allowed a stitch of clothing inside this room." I open the door and step inside.

Eleni looks around the empty hallway, then reaches behind her. she unfastens the ribbon first and the tiny straps slide off her shoulders. Her breasts bounce free, full and begging to be touched. I wait. She unzips the skirt, and the whole dress slips to the floor, leaving her in nothing but heels and a few pieces of jewelry. I palm myself over my pants and step out of the door frame to allow her inside. She glances past me, bites her lip, then bends and picks up the dress before joining me inside.

Smart girl. I shut the door.

"Go to the bedroom and get the black box under the bed. Open it, and pick out your favorites, then wait."

She swallows and walks away. I watch her ass sway and decide I want to take my time. I strip slowly in the entryway, then fold each piece of clothing. Let her wonder what's taking me so long. Let her think about deciding not to wait. I stroke my cock a few times, then stride into the bedroom after her.

She stands in front of the bed with the box of supplies I ordered ahead next to her. I frown.

"You didn't choose anything."

She bites her lip. "They're all my favorites, sir."

A groan pours from my lips. "Such a good girl. Get on the bed." I stride to the box and start pulling out toys.

A shining metal spreader bar with soft leather cuffs. Another set of sparkling nipple clamps. And a length of soft rope in the same blue as her dress. She's going to look beautiful.

The rhythm of set-up comes easily. Adjusting her, adjusting the toys, checking nothing hurts more than it's supposed to. She's pliant, obedient, and so wet I'm actively watching the stain on the bedspread grow. By the time she's ready, my cock aches with the need for release.

I study her in the soft moonlight. The spreader bar holds her opening, exposing her dripping pussy. The nipple clamps dangle from the stiff peaks of her breasts, jingling slightly every time she moves. And the rope, wrapped in complicated patterns I learned long ago, holds her arms together above her head, giving me full access to every inch of her. On a whim, I grab my phone and snap a few pictures.

She moans. I grin.

"Such a good girl for me." I put my phone away and rub my hand over my cock. "Let's test that."

I pull out a final toy, a powerful vibrator, lean it against her clit, and crawl over her to put the tip of my cock against her lips. "Don't come before me."

In one swift motion, I flip on the vibrator and plunge past her lips. She gasps and swallows me down. I groan at the wet, silken heat of her. Restrained, she struggles to find a rhythm, and despite the need in my balls begging me to help her, I remain still. Her frantic blue eyes meet mine, and a moan rumbles over my cock. My control slips. I thrust forward, jamming myself further down her throat and summoning another noise. I wind my fingers into her hair and smile. She's too pretty, all trussed up like this and trying to please me, to stave off my orgasm for long, but based on the frantic wriggling behind me, she doesn't have much time either.

She scrapes her teeth gently over me. My hips snap forward again, and she gags. Tears run down her cheeks, but she taps the side of my leg to signal she's good, so I don't stop. I want her to obey me, and she looks so goddamn good.

Moments before I plunge over the edge, she goes stiff underneath me with another moan as she comes. I force the expression of bliss off my face and pull out. She stares up at me, still caught in the throes of pleasure with the vibrator humming between her legs. Dismissively, I stroke myself the rest of the way and splatter semen all over her chest before her first orgasm even ends. She arches up into the liquid, her breasts shifting and the clamps catching the light, then freezes as she realizes what happened. Her eyes fly open.

"I'm so sorry, sir," she babbles. "I didn't mean to disobey, and—"

I put up a hand to stop her. "You could have done better."

She nods. "I want to be good for you."

I flick off the vibrator. "Prove it."

El blinks. "How?"

I don't answer for a long time. Instead, I play with the clamps on her breasts, enjoying every breathy wince and watching the skin turn pink. I could belt her easily enough, but taking the belt doesn't prove anything other than pain tolerance. No, I want control. After long moments of quiet, I palm my cock. It starts to stiffen. Ready for another round. I saunter over to the nightstand and pull out one of the condoms the hotel provides. A little small, but it'll do. She stares at me with wide eyes and a slightly open mouth, like she's waiting for another blowjob. I roll the protection on and tap her chin.

"You already failed that challenge."

She looks down, embarrassed. "Sorry, sir."

"You're lucky I like you enough to let you try again." I flip her over so her face mashes into the pillows. She struggles against the ropes around her arms for a second, finds no release, and gives up, turning her head to the side. I grab her under the hips and reposition her with her ass in the air, the spreader bar still holding her open. "Same game, pet."

Then, I ram my cock into her weeping pussy. My name tears out of her mouth, halfway to a scream. I grin and set a bruising pace, then reach around to play with one of her dangling breasts. Her moans take on a desperate quality, almost pleading. Fuck, there's nothing quite like a woman who will do anything for you.

A small part of my brain snaps out of domination mode to correct me. There's nothing like a woman who submits to you and challenges you in equal measure. Who turns her obedience over like the most delicious fucking present. I slam my hips into hers and smack her ass just to watch the flesh jiggle. She fucks herself back onto me.

"I'm close," she whimpers.

I grin. "Color?"

"Green," she whines.

I smack her again. "Then too fucking bad."

Her next groan sounds more like a sob as she fights the tide of pleasure. I play her body like an instrument, hitting all the buttons I know drive her insane. Her thighs tremble. Her ass goes pink. Her voice breaks. But she doesn't come.

With a final thrust, my vision whites out, and I spill inside her. A half second later, I hear her near-delirious cry as she releases the flood of pleasure she was holding back.

"Good girl." I fuck her through the aftershocks, then pull out and discard the condom quickly.

When I turn back, El remains splayed on the bed, open and ready for taking. She's still gorgeous. I doubt she could be anything else. But instead of wanting to torture her more, I find myself looking forward to the long, quiet minutes of undoing the restraints and taking care of her in the crash. Watching her become my Eleni again.

I join her in bed.

21

ONE OF THE GIRLS

Eleni

A FEW DAYS after our night in the hotel, I roll over in bed to find the sheets empty. Instead of getting frustrated, I flip the other way and grab my phone. As expected, a text from Dante sits at the top of my notifications.

Piacere all day today. Probably won't be back until late. Dinner?

I type out a quick affirmative and smile. Since I agreed to stay—and agreed to go to Tandon, though there was no way I was going to live on campus—he's obviously been trying. He tells me where he's going, or at least as much as he knows, and offers new plans every time work pulls him away. Butterflies riot in my stomach. I flop onto my back and stare at the ceiling.

Christos made Dante kill him because he got so focused on the prize, he couldn't see anything in his way. That sounded like my brother. As much as I loved—love him, Christos could be a bulldozer. So maybe, just maybe, letting Dante back into my heart isn't a total betrayal of my family.

I get out of bed and ignore the fact I haven't called Mama since I decided not to join her in Greece. I've been spending most of my days trying to catch up on summer reading before the start of the fall semester and helping out with Saints' business here and there, but I've never really paid attention to Piacere. Tony ran it while Dante was healing up. Dante could be doing anything from running guns to napping with his head on his desk all day, and I'd have no idea. Maybe I'll ask if I can go with him someday soon, just see. I pull on a T-shirt and a long, loose skirt. I can always change before Dante gets home, if I want something fancier.

With a few books in hand, I head downstairs, intending to study in the sun on the back porch. As I reach the bottom, the door opens a crack.

"Eleni." Seb stands there, looking exhausted.

"What the hell?" I put the books down and hurry over to check him for injuries.

He shakes his head. "Just know I did everything I could."

That's when I hear the laughter. Shrill and confident and multi-voiced. I have a split second to step back before the door bursts the rest of the way open, and a small army of…women pour inside. I look from Seb to them, trying to figure out what's happening.

"Eleni!" the middle-aged woman in the front squeals, holding her arms out for a hug.

I definitely don't know this woman. "Um, hi?"

"She's Greek, Val. They do things different." Another woman politely elbows her way to the front and sticks her hand out. "Hi, doll. My name's Nicky. Don't mind these harpies, it's just not often we get another one."

I eye the woman's sky-high, bleach-blonde hair, the designer bag dangling from her wrist, the logos stamped across every edge of her tweed skirt-suit. She radiates the energy of someone used to being listened to. But I didn't spend two weeks running this organization to roll over to some PTA mom.

"Eleni." I shake her hand. "One of what?"

"Saints' wives!" Her smile fades a little as she looks me up and down. "You'll fit right in, I'm sure. Let me introduce you to everyone."

Only two weeks of training keeps me from fidgeting with my T-shirt while Nicky introduces me to the whole cadre of women. Italian-sounding names blur into a mass of fitted skirts and shirts so tight I can tell who had a boob job before I finish shaking their hands. I meet Seb's eye over the throng, and he shrugs. I shake my head at him minutely, and he leaves with his shoulders shaking in laughter.

"And last but not least, my Chloe." Nicky pushes the last woman in the group forward. "I hope you don't mind. She's not one of us"—she winks—"but she's been raised in the life, and I've been bringing her around for ages. The meeting just wouldn't feel right without her."

Chloe smiles a little sheepishly and sticks out her hand. I shake it gratefully, thrilled not to be the only twenty-something in the room. She's stunning. Her pale blonde hair, a natural counterpart to her mother's bottled approximation, sweeps up into a simple bun, and she wears a nearly identical suit to Nicky's, but I can tell by the stiffness in her posture that she's either not used to it or hates it. Even with my head spinning, my heart goes out to her a little. It doesn't seem like she wants to be in this meeting any more than I do.

"So, what are we meeting about?" I ask.

Nicky takes my arm and begins leading me through my own house. "Oh my god, I'm so sorry. I thought Dante would've told you. Every year, the Saints throw a barbecue. Just a little get-together for us, and he usually invites the who's-who of bosses. It's time to start planning!"

I don't ask any of these questions as Nicky marches into a sitting room I've literally never used before, and all of the women perch on the various couches like birds on a telephone wire. Tropical birds, based on the color schemes of their various outfits. A wingback chair in the middle of the room remains suspiciously empty, despite Nicky throwing a couple looks at it, so I sit there. As soon as my butt touches the cushion, a flurry of planning breaks out. I just absently nod along, trying not to feel like my world's been turned on its head. These women know Dante and I are only...whatever we are, not married, right? And why the hell have I gone from running the show to bulk-ordering burgers in only a couple weeks?

Mama would know what to do here. I fiddle with my phone. I could call her. But then I'd either have to find a way to tell her about Christos or lie to her about Christos, and I don't know how to do either.

I shoot to my feet. "Does anybody want anything to drink?"

The conversation dies out. Nicky puts a hand on my arm.

"Oh, aren't you sweet." She wrinkles up her nose as she smiles. "Andrea usually makes sure there's sugar-free lemonade ready for us. Chloe, go help her get it."

I need space to breathe. I try to wave her off. "Really, I'm fine—"

Nicky clicks her tongue. "You're Dante's girl. We can't make a decision in the world without you. And Chloe's a good girl, she'd love to help."

Chloe stands, silently underscoring her mother's words. I swallow down my grimace and lead Chloe to the kitchen she probably already knows the way to.

Thankfully, she stays quiet, giving me a second for my own thoughts. Through Dante, I'm in charge of these women. Not because this whole syndicate was mine, but because he fucks me. I pluck at the hem of my T-shirt and try not to seethe. They mean well. I think.

We turn into the kitchen and find Tony there, standing in front of the open fridge.

"When the hell did you get in here?" I ask conversationally. "You don't exactly blend into the crowd."

He starts to turn. "What, you don't think I could pull off—" Tony freezes, swallows. When he speaks again, his voice is softer. "Hey, Chloe. I didn't know you were here."

"Hi." She smiles. "We're planning the barbecue."

He nods and grabs a pitcher of yellow liquid. "Then this would be yours."

I bite my lip and look between them. I've literally never seen Tony stop joking. His tone is softer than I've ever heard it. What's going on?

"I can bring it in," he offers.

"Sure." I shake my head. "Bring some vodka, too. I'm gonna need more than lemonade to survive this."

Tony looks at me, and his smile turns sardonic again. "You think those women share a room without booze? This is already so strong I water it down most of the time."

Chloe giggles behind her hand. He glances at her, then away. I smile to myself as we walk back into the sitting room.

Predictably, Tony's arrival heralds another burst of conversation. The wives tell him how handsome he's gotten, how awful it is that he's not married, how sad it would be if his poor nonna met her maker before she met his wife. I pour myself a hearty glass of lemonade and take a deep breath, then clap.

"I'm sure we'd all love to torture Tony, but this barbecue won't plan itself."

2 2

BRANCHING OUT

Dante

EARLIER THAN EXPECTED, I walk in the front door of my house. Piacere actually ran smoothly for once, and I have high hopes they won't even need me there for another day or two. El and I haven't spent a ton of time together since our day of errands, and I miss her despite falling asleep next to her every night. Sometimes, I think it might be better if she was involved in high-level operations again, but that might just be a side effect of wanting to see her more often.

No, some of the capos still look around for her when I give an order. I know a handful of them text her nearly everything. They'll answer to me—especially because I suspect she told them to—but she's won their loyalty forever. I can't say I don't understand.

I wander through the house until I find Eleni in the living room at the back of the house, sprawled out on the leather couch with a laptop on her chest and a mostly empty pitcher next to her.

"Hey—"

Pitcher. With a little bit of something yellow at the bottom. The wives were here.

"How was your day?" I ask wincingly.

She blows out a long breath and looks at me. "Did you know they were coming today?"

I circle around the couch and sit in front of it, at eye level with her. "I swear, I didn't. I would've warned you."

She sighs again. "They've got a real…energy."

I nodded. "Nicky scares me a little."

Eleni looks at me for a second, then bursts into laughter. "I've watched you walk through a gunfight with a straight face, and she scares you?"

"What?" I put up my hands, grinning at the lightness in her face. "She reminds me of my dad's mom. Scary lady. Just because Nicky doesn't have a wooden spoon yet, doesn't mean she won't get one. The backs of my hands hurt just thinking about it."

That only makes Eleni laugh even harder. My chest warms. It's barely been a week, and already, she looks completely different from the frozen woman I met at the warehouse, my first day back in the world. That time apart left its marks on both of us, but every time I see her smile, healing feels a little more possible.

"What are you up to, then?" I shift to see her laptop screen as her laughter dies out.

The sorts of fitted tops and skirts all the mafia wives wear cover the screen in every shape and color. Bizarrely, my stomach sinks. I don't want her dressed like the other wives.

"I didn't exactly fit in today." She plucks at her oversized T-shirt, then gestures to the skirt I'm pretty sure she told me her mother brought over from Greece.

"I think you look wonderful," I say, trying to figure out why I don't want my gorgeous girlfriend in sexier clothes.

She snorts. "Tell Nicky that."

The pieces click. I don't want to tell anyone about her body. It's so perfect I want to keep it all to myself, under her modest shirts and skirts. The way she hides herself makes her feel so much more like a treasure I'm discovering. Dressing up for the gala or other occasional events is one thing, but I can read the labels of most of the wives' clothing from the outside. I want Eleni to be mine.

But that sounds like something I'd say in bed, not something to admit to in midafternoon daylight. Here, it's possessive. Borderline creepy. I want Eleni to be happy, and if a closet full of spandex makes her happy, I'll figure out how to live with it.

"She wasn't too bossy, was she?" I trail my finger over El's shoulder. "You're supposed to be in charge."

"They were very clear about that." She turns back to her screen. "I don't know how I feel about being in charge of those women just because we're sleeping together."

That stings. "What?"

She shakes her head. "I just mean…I'm good at this. It feels like bullshit that a week ago, the whole city was scared of me, and now I'm a dick-appointed event planner."

I kiss her cheek and sigh. "I know it's not fair. And we'll work on that, I promise. But the barbecue is only a few weeks away. Can you dick-appointedly plan one event so the wives don't tear either of us to shreds?"

She laughs. "You sure have a way with words."

Tony leans into the doorway. "I hate to inter—no, I don't. I have news."

I snort and stand. "Duty calls."

"Dinner at seven?" she asks.

I kiss her on the head as an agreement and leave with my second. He waits until we walk all the way down the hall to my office and I sit to say anything.

"I've been watching Cal like you asked," he says.

I open my laptop and sigh. "So then news would mean you've seen something."

"No, I figured I'd call you in here for a chat. What are you two crazy kids doing for dinner?" He rolls his eyes. "Of course, I've seen something."

I gesture for him to continue and try to fight through the new filters Eleni put on my shit to reach the document I want.

"Cal's smarter than I thought," he says. "At first, I thought he wasn't doing anything more than testing boundaries. A couple of Kings here and there, barely doing anything more than starting fights."

Finally, I open the document. I'm going to need to talk to El about disabling some of these. I know she's the tech whiz, but there's no way these programs are worth how goddamn irritating they are."

"Then I saw the pattern." Tony starts pacing back and forth. "The incursions are all equally spaced out. Geographically, and in time. And they're all on territory the Lombardis or the Coppolas held."

"Multiple Coppola incursions?" I look up. "They barely had more than Benny's."

Tony pauses, inclines his head. "Just two on ex-Coppola turf."

"So, you're telling me another player in the city has been testing the security of newly ceded territory at pretty much exactly the level as to be expected?"

"Yeah," he says slowly. "All right, it's probably normal. The timing just seemed fucked, and I don't trust those Irish bastards as far as I can throw them."

I lean back in my chair. "Me either, Tone, but that's no reason to go inventing conspiracy theories. What if things are actually just quiet?"

He huffs a breath. "I'm not going to stop watching."

"I wouldn't expect you to. Just don't watch so much you piss him off anyway."

Tony scoffs. "What am I, some fucking Cugine?"

I grin. "If you don't have anything else, I'm going to get back to my beautiful girlfriend who spent the day in the clutches of the wives."

Tony nods quickly and, if I didn't know better, hurries out of the room. I stare after him for a second, wondering what the hell lit his ass on fire, then decide he'll tell me if it matters. Eleni waits. Maybe I can convince her to do some other kinds of shopping as well....

I wander out of the office just in time to almost run into her.

"Shit!" She startles back a step. "Sorry, Gianna just texted me. We're going to go shopping for a little before dinner."

I can kill a few hours on my own. I pull out my wallet and hand her the credit card with the highest limit. "Buy whatever you want."

She grins and plucks it out of my fingers. "Done. And I promise I'll be back in time."

With a quick kiss, she disappears upstairs to change, and I head back into my office. Fuck, I need some hobbies.

23

SOMETHING BLUE

Eleni

"WHAT'S WRONG WITH THIS?" I ask as I step out of the dressing room in the fourth outfit since I sent Gianna a few pictures of the clothes I was looking at and she dragged me out for actual shopping.

She sighs. "Real answer?"

I nod. "Clearly, I'm not getting this. It doesn't make any goddamn sense. Why isn't this something one of the wives can wear?"

Gianna stands and walks over to me. "Well, first, you're not one of the wives."

I snort. "Tell them that."

"Trust me, they know." Gianna turns me to the mirror. "But the boss' girlfriend ranks above any actual wife. If you were a mistress… Well, that'd be different. We wouldn't be out in public shopping with Dante's credit card, that's for sure."

I roll my eyes to the ceiling and groan. "How did I go from boss to boss' girlfriend in a week?"

"Dante woke up." Gianna shrugs. "It's not fair, but that's how everyone assumes it works. If you want something different, you're going to have to talk to him, and he's gonna have to convince a bunch of old Italian men to change their minds." She grabs the waist of the jacket and pulls it straight down. "You see this? It's boxy."

"Is boxy bad?" I stare at the fabric. It hides all the parts of me I doubt any of the wives want to get up close and personal with. Plus, I don't really want any of them asking where I got my boob job. The only thing more embarrassing than telling them I didn't would be if I realized they didn't believe me.

"Very." Gianna nods. "And hey, at least you're a girlfriend and you get some say. You could be a comare, like I said. Your skirt is also long."

"Long?" I look at the hem, an inch above my knee, incredulously. "I want to be able to get shit done, don't I?"

"Nope." Gianna smiles. "Or at least you don't want to look like it. You want to like… You got your nails done this morning and spent the rest of the day flirting with the pool boy, okay? This isn't it."

"Maybe I want to be a comare," I grumble.

"All the judgment, none of the power?" Gianna raises one eyebrow. "Trust me, a mafia mistress is not an enviable position."

"Fine." I sigh. "What should I be picking out? I get the feeling this isn't the last time I'm going to see these women."

"Far from it." She drifts off into the nearby racks. "They were just giving you space to settle back in. Now that you're officially a girlfriend with a living boss, I'd expect to spend half your week juggling luncheons, brunches, and teas."

"And college," I say. "And still being a goddamn member because I'm not giving that up either."

Gianna doesn't answer, and I turn back to myself in the mirror. I picked this suit out because it was kind of the same color as Nicky's, but I thought it would suit my eyes. With Gianna's words ringing in my ears, I can only see the issues. It is too big, and kind of old-looking, and everybody would stare at me in this just as much as they did Mama's skirts. Again, I wish I could call her without my stomach rioting and trying to climb out my throat. Mama would know what to say to make me feel like myself again.

"Try this." Gianna reappears with an armful of black and pink fabric. "Best of both worlds."

I accept it and hide away in the dressing room. The pink, such an aggressive neon it's impossible to look away, turns out to be a fitted, silky camisole with black lace on the top. I turn my back to the mirror and pull the top over my head. The suit I was just wearing looked like a bad imitation of Nicky. The navy one crumpled in the corner Gianna had already rejected looked like something Mama would've picked out for me to wear to a college interview. The gray dress next to it was just another color of my funeral dress, something Eleni-before-Dante picked out to look serious. And as much as I tried, the outfits I wore when I was running the Saints still looked like femme Dante. I am different from any of those people now.

Maybe I need to dress differently too.

After the camisole is a pair of pants. Leather pants. My heart almost falls out of my ass, but I squeeze myself into them. Still not looking. I can't until it's done, or I'm going to lose any shred of hope I have.

Finally, I put on the final piece, a black blazer long enough to brush the bottom of my ass with a beautiful, blue floral lining. I shove the sleeves up to my elbows, but they won't stay. Eventually, I give up and fold them, exposing a little of the lining.

My heart hammers. Everything fits like a dream, and I think I could actually move, but I feel really exposed. The pants hug everything, and the camisole hides even less. I take a deep breath, square my shoulders, and march out to see Gianna.

Her jaw drops. My face heats.

"You look incredible," she says, beaming. "Like, beyond. What do you think?"

"I…didn't look," I admit. "I wanted to see your reaction first."

"Well, I think it's basically amazing." She grins.

With another deep breath, I turn.

I don't recognize the woman in the mirror. She looks confident, badass. Unstoppable. Like she could rule the wives and crush Tandon and give Dante a run for his money. Like the person I thought I could be when I was running the Saints.

"I think something's a little off," Gianna says.

I pale. Of course I can't pull this off. I look like a slut.

"Don't freak!" She steps up behind me in the mirror. "I don't know if they have it here, but just consider...."

She drapes a blue scarf over the pink top, and the whole vision *clicks*. My eyes shine. The exposed cuffs make sense. I can already picture the powder-blue heels that'll complete the look.

"The pink was your color," I say quietly.

She nods. "And you're happiest in something a shade or two subtler."

The woman in the mirror doesn't look subtle. She looks like she wears brass knuckles as an accessory. But I want to be her.

"It's perfect," I say.

24

PEACETIME

Eleni

Two hours later, bags fill the back of my car, my deep blue manicure is just dry enough that I'm able to drive myself home, and my hair feels so light that I keep shaking my head back and forth just to feel the curls bounce. Gianna's hairdresser only took off a few inches, enough that it hits my shoulders instead of my mid back, but he added layers that "frame my face," whatever that means, and I feel like a million bucks. I pull into the driveway wearing the first outfit Gianna picked out for me with just a few minutes before dinner at seven.

I race inside and start hunting for Dante. Not in the kitchen. Not in his office. Eventually, the sounds of TV lure me to the living room, where he sits sprawled on the couch, looking bored.

"Hi," I say.

He glances up, then sits fully upright. "Holy shit."

I flush. "Do you like it?"

"Like it?" He leans over the back of the couch. "I think I've had wet dreams about it already."

I laugh. "What did you do while I was gone?"

He groans. "Nothing."

"Nothing?"

He nods glumly, looking suddenly sulky. "This is the side of the mafia you haven't seen yet. Peacetime."

I drop onto the couch next to him. "What's so bad about that?"

"It's boring." He drops his head into my lap.

I card my fingers through his hair. "Well, you weren't always the boss. What did you used to do when there wasn't something to kill or raid?"

"Nothing." He rolls his eyes.

I nudge him. After a moment, he looks up at me.

"I guess that's not quite right," he says. "I used to sit around Piacere and dream about…this. Having someone to do nothing with."

Something in my chest aches. I smile. "That's very sweet."

He chuckles a little self-consciously. "If you want something less sweet, I forgot to arrange anything for dinner."

"How did you keep this place afloat without me?" I tease.

"I didn't." He pulls the camisole aside and presses a kiss to my stomach.

The sensation flutters up through me, and I laugh. "That tickles."

He grins and does it again. I squirm and try to push him off, giggling helplessly, but he holds on. His mouth is hot against my skin, teasing and torturous.

"Stop it!" I laugh.

Dante looks up at me, fire in his dark eyes. "Color?"

My core instantly lights. "Green."

He returns his mouth to my stomach, and the tickling begins anew. I wriggle and shove. The sensation starts to become overwhelming, a new kind of torture that doesn't involve any pain. He lifts my camisole higher, exposes my bra, finds every spot that wrings helpless giggles from my lips. His arms cage me in place, inexorable. He kisses back down my chest, teases the hem of my pants.

"Dante," I pant. "Please."

"You can beg better than that, pet," he murmurs.

Hot need floods me. But not the submissive need to please him. The brass-knuckle need to remind him my obedience is something he earns. I wait, time my move. When he's torturing my ribs, as much as it tickles, his hold loosens. That's my chance.

He returns to the spot once more, and I buck, breaking his hold. I leap up from the couch. He stares at me, hungry and feral.

"Make me," I say.

And then I take off. I sprint through the house with no real destination in mind. Dante's footsteps pound behind me, a promise and a threat. I shiver and wheel around to head upstairs, where the staff tends to go less. Dante's socks slip more than my bare feet, so I gain a second. Once I reach the top landing, a wild impulse overtakes me. I shed my blazer and leave it on the banister. My camisole, I dangle off a doorknob. Dante's door yawns before me, wide open. I drop my bra on the floor as I dodge inside and shut the door.

In the last split second before it opens, I shimmy out of the leather pants and my underwear.

The door bursts open, and Dante flings himself inside, already stripped down to nothing more than his boxers, his cock visibly erect. My heart hammers. He tackles me onto the bed, and we land hard.

"You brat." He backhands me and claims my mouth in a bruising kiss.

I laugh up into him, breathless and free. Whatever punishment he doles out, I've rightly earned, and I'll take it with a smile on my face.

He runs his hands over my ribs, and I shudder with the ghost of his earlier tickling. This time, he's not nearly as gentle. His touch is possessive, sharp. He plucks my nipples, gropes my breasts, all without abandoning my mouth. His teeth split the thin skin of my lips, and coppery blood joins his taste in my mouth. I grin.

"You like this, don't you," he growls. "You act out because you want to be used."

I nod until he pulls back and grabs my jaw.

"If you want to be used, squeeze your tits together."

I obey. He pulls off his boxers, then climbs on top of me and slides his cock between my breasts. The sensation is strange, just to the left of the pleasure I'm looking for, and I toy with my nipples as he fucks me.

"I thought you wanted to be used." He knocks my hands away.

I grin and pluck my nipple again, hissing at the pleasure-pain.

"Disobedient slut." He slaps me again.

The pain sparkles through me, bright and brilliant, and I laugh. That word can't touch me. Nothing can.

"I'm not going to be able to punish you today, am I?" he says.

I shake my head.

"Then there's no reason to deny myself your pretty little pussy." He pulls out of my chest and leans over to the nightstand.

I release my breasts.

He clicks his tongue. "Did I tell you to stop? I deserve the view at least."

I can give him a view. As he slides on a condom with his back to me, I gather my breasts in one arm, displaying them, and spread my lower lips with the other hand. Wetness drips over my fingers, and I pray he's feeling better enough for more than one round. Fuck dinner, I want to eat Dante alive.

He turns back and grins. "Hold that, then, you little slut."

I grin at the challenge, and he slams his cock into me without another word. The sudden stretch burns just a little, and I laugh. His hips press my hand against my clit, increasing the pleasure. I play with my nipples as much as I can.

"Fuck, you're hot." He scrabbles toward the nightstand for a second, then pulls out an old-fashioned Polaroid camera. "I picked this up after your little reaction last time. Thought you might want to see yourself from my perspective."

As he rams into me, the flash goes off. A photo shoots from the front of the camera and rains down onto me. I don't grab it. I won't lose that easily. I keep myself open as Dante takes picture after picture of me, splayed out on our bed without a care in the world. He never loses rhythm, slamming my hand into my clit. My orgasm arrives between snaps of the lens, in strobing technicolor, every second captured until Dante follows me over the edge.

I don't even let him pull out before I'm kissing him again. We're nowhere near done.

2 5

REGRETS

Eleni

BY THE TIME I finally topple off Dante, sated, the sun is nowhere to be seen, and dinner is long forgotten. My skin clings to the sheets with sweat, and I spend a long time just catching my breath.

After that long time passes, I look over at Dante. Tonight wasn't our most intense session, but usually by this point, he's up reminding me aftercare is an important part of the process and I'll get a UTI if I don't go to the bathroom. Instead, he just lays on the pillow, breathing heavily and staring at the ceiling with his gaze distant. Judging by the wrinkle between his eyebrows, business has him worried, not me.

Maybe this is where I fit into the Saints now. Not boss in name, but boss in bed. The place he comes to unload the problems he can't figure out on his own, and I help him unsnarl them. At least for now.

"Thought for a thought?" I graze my fingers down the middle of his chest, avoiding the few remaining staples he says Dr. Domino is going to take out in a couple days. The stitches have all melted into his skin, leaving behind an angry red scar.

He sighs. "I was thinking about what I would have done differently, that day in the Greek Corner, if I knew we were going to end up here."

I frown. "I wouldn't have done anything differently there."

"I know that." He takes my hand and smiles softly at me. "You're happy, aren't you?"

"Yeah." I look at him. "There are a few things we still need to work out, and I need my place in this organization to make sense, but over-all…yeah. Are you not?"

"With you, always." He kisses the back of my hand. "But I think that might be selfish. I think you might've been better off if I never opened this door, fell in love with you, and dragged you into my fucked-up world."

"I wasn't exactly on the outside of it," I say, trying to rectify the softness in his eyes with his return to the completely condescending opinion that he's the only reason I'm here. "Why is it so bad for me to be here?"

He smiles softly. "You make me dangerous."

I raise an eyebrow.

"More dangerous," he concedes. "There are things I'm willing to do, to risk, that I wouldn't before, just to make sure you're safe and happy. I'm not sure there isn't a line I wouldn't cross for you anymore."

"With me," I correct. "You're not alone in this now. I know this business, and I'm here with you."

He meets my gaze, his dark eyes heavy. "You are as good as most of my capos and better than the rest. You might be better than me. But it will always be different for women in this world. There are things my—our enemies will be willing to do to you that they'd never do to me. So I need you to know that there might be a day when I tell you to run and hide, and I need you to listen on that day."

His words, and the worry underpinning them, settle into me. Memories of Luca, of the way all the Lombardi guys talked to me, float to the forefront of my mind. I can't exactly imagine Luca teasing Dante's mouth with a gun. In this game, men are always going to see me as something sexual, no matter how I dress or what I do. It's infuriating, but it's not Dante's fault.

"What about you?" he says. "I was promised a thought for a thought."

I smile. "I'm thinking I still wouldn't change anything."

"Anything?" He rolls onto his side to face me.

"Most of the worst parts weren't my fault," I say, hearing the words for the first time. "There's nothing I could've done to stop Frank Lombardi from killing Baba. Or you from killing Christos."

Dante exhales slowly. I haven't said those words to him yet. He's hurt by them, obviously, but like he regrets it. Like he wishes Christos was still alive as much as I do.

"I do wish Mama was here," I admit. "I know it's too dangerous, and I don't mind that, but I miss her."

Dante kisses my knuckles. "We'll visit her soon. Peacetime leaves a lot more space for vacation."

"I'll hold you to that." I smile.

"I expect you to." He sits up. "Now come on. If you don't go to the bathroom, you're going to get a UTI."

I laugh as I obey. There he is.

WHEN THE AFTERCARE IS DONE, Dante collapses into bed and falls asleep before he even hits the pillow. I pull a T-shirt over my naked body and pad downstairs for a water refill. The bottle by the bed is dangerously low, but he needs his sleep. He's trying to be tough, but the injury in his side is still healing. His stamina was flagging even tonight.

On my way, I noticed the light in Dante's office is still on. May as well get that while I'm up. The house staff knows not to go in except on the specified cleaning days.

I lean in and realize one of his desk drawers is still open. I shake my head. There's no one quite like him for blowing into a room and back out with no idea of the mess he leaves behind. He had the same effect on me that first day at the Greek Corner. I walk over to the desk to close the drawer.

On the top of his scattered stationery sits an unmistakable velvet box, just the size for a ring. My heart leaps into my throat. I shut the desk drawer harder than I need to, hurry to the door, shut off the light, and leave. That's just the ring from the jeweler, right? The tracking one we talked about?

Or is Dante planning on proposing?

26

FRIENDS CLOSE

Dante

A FEW DAYS LATER, I lean on my horn as the car in front of me completely ignores the green light overhead. "What the fuck do you mean, am I sure we have to do this?"

Tony rolls his eyes. "Exactly what I goddamn said. I know ignoring Cal Duncan isn't smart, but just because he called the meeting doesn't mean we have to do it in his home fucking base."

"You'd prefer neutral territory." I speed forward as the car finally moves and dodge around them to reach the open road ahead. "Like Chinatown?'

"You're in a rare mood," he grumbles. "Thought I was supposed to be the fucking funny one."

"I thought so too." I grin at my old friend. "And I'm just trying not to walk into an out-of-the-blue meeting with Cal Duncan looking like we're crying over spilled milk. Didn't you say he was minding his Ps and Qs?"

"Technically." Tony shakes his head. "As technically as a motherfucker could. He's dancing right on the edge of our territory, just barely not starting something."

I pull up in front of McCreegan's Pub, up in Woodlawn in the Bronx. It's a hole in the wall place, just a few steps up from Benny's. I shake my head. No one in this goddamn city has any panache other than me. Tony grunts in agreement. I park the car, and we get out and walk inside.

Of course, inside isn't much better. The place looks like it was transplanted right from Ireland, complete with a massive, stained, dark-wood bar and the smell of a thousand years of old beer. I dodge between a couple tables of old Irish men drinking in the middle of the day and saunter up to the bar.

"The Lucky Charm," I say with an eye roll.

The bartender nods and disappears, then returns a few minutes later.

"You're late," he says.

"Traffic," Tony replies.

The bartender grits his teeth but leads us through a swinging door into the kitchen, then into the freezer.

"Did Cal decide to kill us after all?" I rub my arms, trying not to turn into an icicle.

The bartender ignores me to shoulder-check a particularly frost-bitten box. It slides back into the wall with a click, and then the whole wall swings open like a door.

With a relieved sigh, I step through, expecting something more modern. Behind the freezer wall stands what looks for a second like a replica of the bar out front, just a little cleaner. Then, I realize the redhead behind the bar here is none other than Cal Duncan himself.

"Gentlemen!" he calls. "Please, come in, warm up."

He begins pouring three mugs of beer so dark it looks like liquid mud. Fucking hospitality rules. I'll have to drink the swill. One glance at Tony tells me he's thinking the same goddamn thing. Still, we sit on the barstools and accept the drinks.

"Slainte." Cal raises his own beer and drinks

I grip the handle of my mug and take a pull. Swamp water, with bits of swamp floating it in. I smile and set it back down.

"Surprised to see you swapped out the old ball and chain." Cal grins and sticks out his hand. "Tony? We spoke on the phone. You look exactly how I pictured."

Tony shakes his hand tensely. "Right back 'atcha."

Cal turns back to me. "So, when can I expect the wedding invitation? She seemed quite enamored of you the other day."

"About the time I can expect the topic of this conversation, it seems," I say.

He laughs uproariously. "Well, the Irish are blunt, but it seems we've got nothing on you."

"Apologies for my bluntness. I'm rather busy with the barbecue, which you did get an invitation to. And, to be frank, I'm not much interested in doing business with you."

"You think our problems start and end with a couple partnerships?" He laughs again. "We're in deep shit, my fine friend. Federal shit."

My stomach drops. "That hasn't popped up on our radar, and we have people inside most of the major agencies."

"That's because you're not looking for people, you're looking for a person." Cal sips his own beer. "One Special Agent Henry Alcott, to be precise. And he might not be on your particular radar because, to hear tell, he's your stock." He smiles. "Saint stock."

I blink and glance at Tony out of the corner of my eye. We know Henry. Hell, Tony's nonna's Christmas Eve used to include Henry Alcott. His grandfather was a Saint. I have a vivid memory of passing him the seventh fish one year, only for him to take one look at it and sprint from the room to throw up because he was sneaking beer all night. He hasn't been by the last few years though.

"Let's say I believe you." I trace the handle of my mug. "Why the fuck would it benefit you to tell us this? Is there more you're holding back for a price."

"I'm an open book." Cal spreads his arms. "Truth told, I don't think we need any more shaking up here in the city, and rats have a tendency to do some shaking."

I study him for a long moment. I know Cal Duncan by reputation mostly. Men don't get to our position without a few secrets, but I know what sort of man Cal is. The bravado's his favorite cover, a game that unnerves all the men like me, who he thinks have sticks up our asses. But there's a not-quite-playful flicker in his eyebrows, a shred of nervous energy in the way he spins his beer around.

"This city is a house of cards," I say slowly. "And if our cards tumble, yours are next. Someone's breathing down your neck. The Russians?"

Cal grins too wide. "Handsome and smart. Your girl must be pleased."

I stand. "Thanks for the beers, Cal, but you don't need to worry about Henry Alcott."

"I think that's mighty short-sighted, gentlemen." His smile doesn't fade. "The Russians aren't just sniffing my neck of the woods."

I nod to Tony, who stands.

"We'll see you at the barbecue." I turn and walk back out the freezer, through the front pub, and don't even pause until we reach the car. Tony walks at my side in perfect silence.

"Fucking Henry," he says as soon as he drops into the passenger's seat.

"Fucking Henry," I agree. "Look into it, okay? And maybe check to see if Cal's telling the truth about the Russians. The last thing we need is them sneaking up on us."

Tony nods. "I've never liked rats."

27

ENEMIES CLOSER

Eleni

I STARE at the scene around me in something between surprise and horror.

This is Dante's backyard. I look up and see his house looming over the party. But instead of the yard being filled with gunfire or hushed conversation, classic rock blares from a pair of speakers. Dante himself stands at the grill, flipping burgers and nursing a light beer I've never seen him drink before. Tony and a couple other capos hold court by the grill. A few East Asian men Dante warned me when they walked in were representatives of the triads chat with some Saints soldiers. Cal Duncan stands alone by the pool, holding a bottle of dark beer he brought and surveying the scene. I turn away, toward the platter of watermelon salad—whatever the fuck that is—before his gaze can alight on me. Still, it looks like something out of a coming-of-age movie, not a tense meeting between some of the most dangerous men in New York City.

The only concession to normalcy is the color palette of Dante's outfit. Sure, he's wearing cargo shorts laden with grill tools and the remote for the speakers, as well as a short-sleeved button down that dances terrifyingly close to the Hawaiian shirt line, but all of it is blessedly black. It feels like an anchor in a surreal storm.

Nicky breezes up to me in a skin-tight white sundress with a passel of wives in tow. I adjust my romper, a dark charcoal to compliment Dante's outfit, which fits me tighter than any single piece of clothing I've ever owned but gives me more maneuverability than her dress allows.

"Eleni!" She throws her arms out for a hug.

I hug her back. After a few weeks of barbecue meetings, the embrace has become non-negotiable.

"Aren't you so cute." She releases me. "You two are a matched set these days, huh?"

I shrug. "I wanted people to be able to pick me out of the crowd."

"You and me both." Val squeezes me and passes me down the line. "So, has he popped the question yet?"

My stomach drops to my toes. Dante hasn't breathed a word about the ring box I found, which seems really weird if it's just the ring we already talked about. Could the wives know more than I do?

"Oh, ignore her." Nicky rolls her eyes. "Val is just a gossip monger. If you're not ready, you're not ready."

"I'm—"

"No, what she should really be asking about is kids," Nicky continues. "Obviously, you'll get married when you do, but it's never too early to start thinking about school districts."

"School districts?" Val screeches. "God, Nicky, you'll move them to Scarsdale before she even knows he's serious."

"Oh, like Dante would've gone this far if he wasn't—"

I close my eyes and let their bickering fade into the background, another skill I've developed over the weeks of meetings. Mama and Baba would've loved this. The first few years, they tried to throw a Fourth of July party to "have the real American experience," but none of the other Greek immigrants they made friends with really cared.

After three years of Christos and I sitting sullenly next to a melting red-white-and-blue cake we both refused to eat, they gave up, and we just watched the fireworks every year instead. If Mama was here right now, no one's drink would get lower than a few sips deep before she'd already refilled it, and she'd still find time to bother Dante about his grilling technique. I allow myself a small smile. Maybe next year.

The bickering abruptly falls silent, and I open my eyes. A stunning woman maybe a decade older than me with long, cornsilk-blonde hair looks around the backyard.

"Oh my god," Nicky whispers. "I didn't think she'd come."

"She's got some *coglioni*." Val snickers.

"Who is that?" I ask, watching her float through the backyard, talking to this group and that. Everyone seems to light up at her arrival.

"Camila Donato." Nicky smiles conspiratorially. "The widow Marco, one of Enzo's capos."

It takes me a second to connect the name "Enzo" with Dante's father, partially because Camila looks more like she's Dante's age than his dad's.

"Why is it weird that she's here?" I ask.

"Don't worry, doll, it's all rumor." Nicky puts an arm around my shoulders and turns me away from Camila. "All you need to know is she gets taken care of like a made man's woman deserves. Apartment in the city, spending money, all courtesy of…the Saints."

More snickers break out. I whip back to look at the other wives, and Camila catches my attention again. She's wearing a simple, floral sundress, but something about the fabric or the cut makes her look like she's caught in her own private music video, the wind tousling skirt and hair in perfect unison.

"The girl deserves to know the truth," Val says with a click of her tongue. "The rumors say she killed Marco. And he wasn't even hitting her or nothing."

"Val!" Nicky says. "If that were true, she wouldn't be a kept woman."

As I watch, Dante looks up from the grill and notices Camila. A smirk floats across his expression. When I turn back to Camila, I catch the ghost of a smirk on her lips before she notices me. She looks me up and down with icy grace, and something sick shivers down my spine.

I don't like Camila.

Dante flips a burger, then shuts the lid and strides across the lawn toward me. Nicky releases me quickly enough that Dante doesn't even have to pause before sliding his arm around my waist.

"All right, folks, grub's up in a second." He raises his cup. "But first, I'd like to give a toast. Usually, I brag about how well we're doing, what we can look forward to in the upcoming year." He grins down at me. "But this time, I want to brag about this woman right here. Eleni is a tribute to the Saints, a literal lifesaver, and someone I'm so happy to call mine."

He dips me into a kiss, and people whoop. But when he tips me back onto my feet, laughing, I can't help but notice Camila is staring at us.

No, not us. Dante. With a predatory look in her green eyes.

2 8

WHAT AM I MISSING?

Eleni

SUNSET HAS COME and gone by the time the last guests leave.

After the grilling, everyone loitered, eating classic American food and listening to classic American music, until darkness finally fell. Then Dante, giggling like a kid, disappeared with Seb and Tony. They reappeared minutes later with an unlabeled box and proceeded to light off the least legitimate fireworks show I could have expected. Some didn't light. Others fell off their little post. I laughed the whole time, and they handed out sparklers at the end.

That, at least, felt like the summers I knew, waiting until the tiny fires threatened the top of my hand before dropping it on concrete and stamping it out. The only thing missing was Christos, trying to convince me to sword fight him. Luckily, it only took one mention before Seb was happy to accept the challenge. As always, our sparklers shattered instantly. It wouldn't have been right if they didn't

After everything is cleaned up, Dante and I stumble upstairs. Well, Dante stumbles. Apparently, he avoids those beers because he's much worse at judging his tolerance with them. I catch him as he threatens to fall down the stairs again, and he bursts into laughter.

"God, I love you," he says.

I smile. "I'd love you a lot more if you could walk your own ass up the stairs."

His mouth falls open dramatically. "Rude!"

Then, he spanks my ass and scampers up the last few steps. I follow him with a laugh. If he was like this in college, I can see what Tony was talking about. It's easy to imagine him surrounded by giggling coeds. I climb the last few steps and feel a little wobble from the few glasses of lemonade I had. Dante winks at me, then races ahead to his bedroom at the end of the hall.

"Slow down!" I call. "I thought you wanted me to sleep with you."

Dante wheels around and runs all the way back, then slips an arm around my waist. "Fuck yes I do."

I nudge him. "I meant *sleep* in your bed."

He pouts, and I can't help but laugh. Just to be difficult, I walk the hallway as slowly as I can, and Dante wheedles me to speed up the whole way to the door. When we finally reach it, he darts ahead again and sits on the bed.

"Go on," he says.

I laugh and indulge him by reaching for the zipper of my romper. Suddenly, I remember Camila walking into the party, the way she stared at me.

"Did you talk to Camila today?" I ask.

Dante blinks a few times, and a little of the drunkenness clears from his expression. "Briefly. Who told you about her?"

I shake my head, fiddling with the zipper. "Just Nicky. She said she was a widow or something?"

"Uh, yeah." He reaches out and runs a hand over the curve of my hip. "I'm happy to answer your questions, but does it have to be now?"

"You're right, I'm sorry." I bite my lip and pull the zipper down an inch. "Just…well, did you invite her?"

He laughs. "El, I don't actually invite anyone. Nicky handles the social side, Tony the business. I was surprised she showed up, but just because she's been kind of distant lately. Now, please…?"

I look at him for a moment. There's no worry in his eyes, no furrow between his eyebrows, no obvious sign he's hiding something. But I can't shake the weird feelings churning in my stomach. Maybe Camila is the only one who knows the truth. Or maybe there's something hiding behind his *been kind of distant.*

"It's just that—"

Dante drops to his knees in front of me and presses a kiss to my lower thigh. "Tomorrow, I promise, I'll let you interrogate me for an hour. Advanced techniques and everything. But right now, I'm tipsy and horny, and you're fucking gorgeous."

I've always struggled to resist Dante. But on his knees, begging for the chance to have sex with me? I melt like the ice cream this afternoon.

"Tell me what you want." I card my fingers through his hair.

He kisses a little higher up my leg. "Take off the fucking romper."

I remain still, waiting to see if he returns to his begging.

Dante growls and sinks his teeth even higher up my leg, just below the hem of the shorts. "I'm done asking nicely."

I grab his hair and yank him back. "I'll go sleep in my old room if that's how you're going to behave."

His eyes darken. My heartbeat drops between my legs as I realize I've unlocked the feral side of him. But I don't release his hair. I want my Dante back.

Dante doesn't try to break my hold. Instead, he just stands slowly, making me feel every inch he has over me. I raise onto my tippy-toes, and my arm still strains to hold on.

"I think the barbecue spoiled you, pet," he murmurs. "Made you forget exactly who I am."

I swallow. "Remind me."

He grabs me around the waist and throws me back onto the bed. I lose my grip on his hair almost instantly. Before the mattress stops bouncing, he's on his knees in front of me again, throwing my legs over his shoulders. He pulls aside the crotch of my romper and underwear in one smooth move and presses his mouth to my pussy.

I moan, even more wetness flooding to meet him. He circles my clit, teases my entrance. I grab the sheets and squirm. Dante fits his hand in between us, fucks one finger inside me. The sudden stretch makes me gasp. A second digit threatens. Tonight is not the kind of night when I get room to breathe. I roll my hips against him, crushing his nose, wringing pleasure out before he takes more from me. Noises pour from my lips in a hapless waterfall.

He pulls back. "Who do you belong to?"

I nearly scream as his fingers still and my orgasm melts out of my grasp. He slaps my face.

"Incorrect. You get one more try, pet."

My chest rises and falls with frantic breaths. His night-dark eyes sear. It would be so easy to give him what he wants. Pleasure curls at the edges of my vision. Strange emotions churn my stomach.

"No one." I smirk down at him. "The man who used to own me disappeared at a barbecue today."

Something white-hot fills Dante's gaze, and anticipation slicks my thighs.

29

YOURS

Eleni

My breath catches as Dante looks me over like he's deciding how to ruin me first. I've pushed him to the brink, to the wild place I know scares him sometimes. But tonight, I need that. He has to remind me who he is.

The calm before the storm ends abruptly, with Dante grabbing the top of my romper and yanking. The thin straps can't hold up against his strength. They snap, and my breasts bounce free as the strapless bra I had to wear slides down with the rest of the fabric.

I gasp. "I liked that."

"I'll buy you more." He keeps pulling, dragging the ruined garment down my body. In seconds, I'm naked. "That's my right, because you're mine."

I swallow. "I'm—"

He slaps one of my breasts with a spark of pain. "You'll stop talking if you know what's good for you, pet."

"And if I don't?" My voice shakes a little. I tremble with want.

He cups my pussy harshly, dragging his fingers through my wetness and coaxing the embers of my lost orgasm back to life. "You're determined to find out, aren't you?"

I can't do anything but let my mouth fall slack. Needy breaths hiss from my lips.

"You're such a slut." He shakes his head. "Come on."

He yanks me up off the bed. I stumble to my feet but pause when he reaches the door to the balcony.

"Where are we going?" I ask.

"Wherever I damn well please." His grip on me tightens, inexorable. He flings open the door, and cool night air washes over my bare body. Soft conversation from the few staff members still cleaning up the yard floats up.

"They're going to—"

"Good." He throws me down onto a plush lounge chair. "If you don't know you're mine, at least someone else will."

I glance over the railing. "But I have to—"

"You have to earn an orgasm, pet." Dante stares down at me. "Nothing else. How would you like to do that?"

I force my gaze away from the people below. His instructions are clear, and I've pushed him to a point where I can't argue with anything but a safe word.

And, if I'm being perfectly honest, I don't want to stop.

"I could suck your cock," I say.

"Do better," Dante replies.

Fuck. I bite my lip. "I'll do it sitting on the railing."

He hums. "Getting there."

"With the lights on," I say desperately.

He grins. Oh, god, what have I done? He flicks on the balcony lights, casting my pale skin in brilliant light. I boost myself up onto the lower railing, making sure the upper one supports my back, and he pulls out his cock. He's basically fully dressed. I'm bare-assed where anyone could see. I open my mouth and swallow him down.

Like this, it's easy to lose myself in him. He surrounds me. He's all I can see, hear, taste. He grabs my hair and rams me forward. I relax my throat and accept every inch of him with a moan. He hisses through his teeth, and I pull back to set the rhythm.

Not tonight. He yanks me back, fucking my mouth at whatever pace he wants. I can do nothing but relax and become a vessel for his pleasure. I run my tongue along the underside of his shaft, play with his balls, tease my own nipples as I melt deeper into the moment. Time disappears. I don't even notice the murmured warning, seconds before he crushes my nose into his pubic hair and spills down my throat.

I swallow as fast as I can, savoring the taste of him, but when he pulls out, one vulgar string of come connects my lips to his cock in the shining light.

"Who do you belong to?" he asks.

I'm not done. I tap the head of his softening cock. "Him."

Dante snarls and spins me around so my breasts hang freely over the railing. The rough stone scrapes my ribs, and I moan. I don't know if anyone is still down there. I don't want to. I shut my eyes.

He pushes his thumb inside me and fucks me lazily. "Stay here."

Footsteps and the rattle of a door tell me he went back inside and shut me out. Wetness drips down my thighs at the thought of being left here, made to greet the dawn as punishment for my insolence. In my imagination, Dante would return in the morning, only to edge me a few times and make me go about my normal day. As the minutes tick on, I start to wonder if I might be right.

Finally, the door opens again.

"As expected," Dante says. "Being displayed like this only makes you needier. Because you know it's a sign of who you belong to."

I shake my head. He slaps my ass.

"I know you're a brat. Spread your legs."

That, I'm happy to obey. Some cool and bulbous presses against my asshole, and Dante leans over me, the brush of skin on skin revealing he stripped during his absence.

"This is a reminder," he says. "I want you to keep it in all day tomorrow."

I whine. We haven't tried this yet, but whatever he has against my ass drips with sticky lube. "Green."

Dante presses the object forward, and I try to relax. As it widens, I realize it's one of the butt plugs he showed me. My tight muscles ache at the intrusion, and I pant. Dante traces a finger over my clit, a white-hot distraction. I inhale shakily.

And the plug slips in. Dante swears quietly. I adjust to the new feeling of fullness, of heaviness. He has to fuck me now, right?

He trails something else over my pussy. It's warm, and wet, but not shaped like one of his fingers.

"Do you feel me, pet?" he asks.

His cock. I've never felt it bare down there. I haven't had time to get on birth control. Wild with want, I rock back into him.

"Greedy." He spanks me hard enough that I can feel my ass wobble around the plug. "You can't have that."

I keen, high and unselfconscious, as the unmistakable sound of a condom opening fills the air. A moment later, he lines himself up again, now covered.

"If you want to come," he whispers. "Tell everyone who you belong to."

He slams into me. The feeling of fullness doubles, his cock pressing against the plug in my ass, the only thing I'm wearing. I moan. All thought of disobedience melts out of me. Of course I'm his. I don't want to be anything else.

"Dante," I pant.

"Better, pet." He grabs my hips and fucks me hard enough I can feel the bruises purpling my skin. "Keep going."

"I belong to you, sir." My breasts swing freely, completely exposed. I don't care.

"More."

My ruined orgasm flares back to life, teetering on the edge already after so much teasing.

"I belong to you, Dante," I moan.

He chuckles low in his throat and circles my clit. Oh, god, I'm so close.

"Dante!" I scream. "I'm yours!"

I careen over the edge into brilliant pleasure. He fucks me slowly, drawing out the aftershocks. Dante's touch gentles, and I realize something important. He's mine, too.

3 0

HOMESICK

Eleni

A COUPLE DAYS LATER, I close one of my assigned readings and check the time. Too early for lunch. Too late to start something new. I glance at my phone, sitting on the couch next to me in the living room. I've been missing Mama a lot lately. Maybe… Maybe one call won't hurt.

I'm dialing almost before I finish the thought. My heart hammers. What am I going to tell her if she asks about Christos? Or Dante?

She picks up after a few rings. "Hello? Who is—"

"Mama!" I squeal.

"*Zouzouni?*" she asks disbelievingly. "I thought—I mean, I feared—"

"I'm all right, Mama," I say. "Safe and sound."

Her broken sob crackles through the phone. "Why did you not call sooner? Oh, I was so worried."

"I'm sorry, Mama." Tears sting my own eyes, and I wish she was here to hug. "It wasn't safe."

"To call? That Dante lies to you," she says. "It is always safe to call your mama."

I know that's not true after my weeks in the boss' chair, but I don't disagree with her. "How are you? I want to hear everything."

"Pah! You want to hear about me after all this time?" I can picture her shaking her head. "*Ohi.* You first, *zouzouni.*"

I tell her…not everything, but a lot. That I got into the Tandon Institute, which earns gasps and cheers. That I killed Luca, which earns gasps and a few more tears. That Dante and I are something, which earns gasps and a lecture on making sure I'm safe with my heart and my body. I poke one of the dark bruises hidden under my shirt and make a mental note to be careful when Mama comes home. Nothing about Cal Duncan, who seems to have ceased nosing around since the barbecue, or my time as boss. My time as a Saint at all, really. Or Christos.

Mama murmured a soft prayer. "So much in so little time."

"You can say that again." I sit back in my chair and sigh. "But I've missed you, Mama. How are things in Parikia?"

"Things are…." She mutters something. "Things are Adriani. She brings drama with her wherever she goes. I cannot make friends with a neighbor but she hates them, cannot strike up a conversation in the market but she is refused service."

I laugh and start to settle in for a longer conversation. "Refused service? You have to—"

Footsteps sound in the hallway behind me. I turn and see Gianna, still wearing her makeup from dancing last night in smeary streaks. My heart sinks.

"Can I call you back, Mama?"

"Oh. Yes, of course. Call often. Make your…mafioso pay the international bills," she says.

"I will." I mean it, too. My chest aches just hearing her voice. I've missed her more than I realized. After a few more goodbyes, I finally hang up.

Gianna has taken one of the armchairs in the room. "I'm freaking out over nothing. You should call your mom back."

I smudge a thumb over her cheek and show her the layer of blush and sparkles that comes back. "If you wanted me to think you were fine, you should've showered."

She laughs, though the sound has a manic edge, and stands. "Really, I shouldn't have come here. I don't know if he—"

"He?" I ask.

She flinches. Goose bumps break out across my skin. Nothing scares Gianna like this, and certainly not some man. I grab her wrist and pull her onto the couch with me.

"You have to tell me."

She inhales shakily. "I'm probably just being paranoid. But I was dancing last night—"

I bite back the word "obviously."

"—and this new guy showed up. I assume everything's normal, dance up on him like usual, but there's something in the back of my head saying I recognize him. I ignore it. I meet a lot of guys. So anyway, he pays for a private dance."

I grin. From my time as the boss, I know the money on those is good.

"Right? I was thrilled." She runs a hand through her long hair. "But once we get in there, he just wants to talk. That happens too sometimes, but his questions were…weird. Like, he wanted to know about my dad, and who owned the club, and why all the security was clustered around one random backroom." She raises her eyebrows at me.

I nod, then shake my head. "I'm not following."

"*Ithinkhewasacop,*" she blurts.

I reel back. "You have to tell—fuck. Dante's gone for the day. He might be at Piacere?"

She shakes her head. "I might've checked there first."

"And scared the shit out of Carla looking like that, I bet." I rub her shoulder, my mind whirring. A cop. I haven't been super involved in the Saints day-to-day, too busy getting ready for Tandon, but this is important. This is a red-alert situation. "Okay, here's what we're going to do. You're going to come upstairs with me and shower. While you're doing that, I'll text everyone who might know where

Dante is. And if I haven't found him by the time you get out, you and I are going on a boss hunt."

She nods. "So you don't think I'm just losing it?"

"Of course not." I smile. "Not that I'm always the best judge of that. But I'd rather cry cop when there's no cop than miss something."

"Yeah. Of course." She smiles and already looks a little steadier, like just admitting what happened helped.

I lead her upstairs and text all the capos who update me most often about Dante while she showers. But Gianna takes a long time in the shower, and sending texts doesn't take long at all. Eventually, my mind drifts away from the cop and to her repeated questioning of whether she was just freaking out.

"Hey, can I ask you something?" I yell over the spray.

"Can't hear you," she calls back. "Come in!"

I open the door slowly. I know this happens in movies, but I've never really had a "talk to me while I'm in the shower" level friend. The curtain hides everything of her but an outline. I sit on the toilet and stare at the wall anyway.

"So Camila showed up to the barbecue," I say.

She whistles. "Lemme guess, you got the wives' version of events?"

"I certainly got an earful." I smile wryly. "Do you know her?"

"By reputation mostly. Why do you ask?"

"Because I want to know if I'm just freaking out." I sigh. "When she walked in, I thought—"

The door opens downstairs. I shoot up.

"Eleni?" Seb calls.

3 1

OLD FRIENDS

Dante

I TRUDGE into Piacere as the sun starts to dip low in the sky. Long day
at the docks today. It needed to be done—some of my foremen get
uppity if I don't check in often enough—but fuck, I hate docks days.
The regular LEDs cast my club in an unattractive light, destroying all
the magic. I shamble past janitors cleaning up and dancers in sweats
practicing routines on the poles. I'm actually looking forward to the
paperwork awaiting me downstairs because it means I get to sit my
ass down for a second.

On a whim, I pause at the bar and wait for Carla to walk over.

"Send a glass of scotch down to my office." I think for a moment.
"Maybe just send the decanter."

My club manager nods sharply. "The decanter would be smart.
You have a guest."

"A guest?" My eyebrows shoot up. "Who the hell did you let into
my office?"

"A woman who swore up and down she knew you." Carla raises
her hands defensively. "She had the phrase."

I spin away from the bar and scowl as I storm down to my office. The phrase had been a fucking stupid idea. Anybody who knew the right words to say gained access to my office without Carla having to call me for every approval. In concept, it streamlined her day. In practice, it was stupid spy-movie shit I didn't know how to get rid of. I opened the door to my office.

One of the chairs across from my desk spun slowly around to reveal its occupant. Camila, in a pure-white suit with no shirt under the jacket. My frustration melts into tiredness. I forgot I gave her the phrase. No red alert. I drop into my chair behind my desk, and my muscles groan as they finally relax.

"What brings you out of the city?" I ask. "We're not hiring for dancers right now."

She laughs, a high, clear sound. "You're sweet. I don't know if anyone is hiring dancers my age."

I wave her words away. "You're barely thirty. I think you look as beautiful as the first day I saw you in my father's club. With the right lighting, you could go from a widow to a mobster's wife again in no time."

She shakes her head in mock hurt. "You know just how to make a lady feel special. What kept you out so long?"

"Work." I rub the back of my neck. "What else? You weren't waiting long, were you? You can text me."

"You're sweet, but it wasn't that long." She stands and holds up her hands. "Do you mind? I've been told I have magic fingers."

I roll my eyes. "I told you that, and I was drunk."

"Still." She waggles her fingers.

I hesitate. Camila really is as beautiful as I remember. But a shoulder massage doesn't mean anything, especially when I don't want anything to do with anyone other than Eleni. And she was great at those. I nod.

She circles around behind me and begins working knots out of my muscles. "I was just swinging by to catch up. The organization looks good. Though there were a few new faces at that barbecue."

"Yeah, recruitment is up," I say. "A little to the left."

She obeys immediately. Always did. "I couldn't help but notice you've got a new woman in your life."

"That I do," I say slowly.

"Where did you meet her?"

"Her family got caught under the Lombardi's thumb." It's a true enough story, and all Camila needs to know. "I pulled her out, and she stuck."

"Stuck," she repeats. "Not very romantic."

"I didn't mean—"

Camila laughs. "I'm just teasing. She's cute. A little young. Has she even graduated?"

"Her schooling got delayed," I say. "But she's entering the Tandon Institute in the fall." I squirm under her hands. "How are things with you?"

"Oh fine, fine," she says breezily. "Tandon is impressive. What's she majoring in?"

This is starting to feel like a cat-and-mouse game, and I've never liked being the mouse. "Why did you come to the barbecue? I thought you were done with those."

"Curiosity." She digs hard enough into a knot that I can feel her acrylic nails. "I wanted to know what shiny new toy pulled your attention away."

I shake off her hands and shove my chair back, making her skitter away to avoid being hit. "Eleni isn't a toy."

"She could've fooled me, in that outfit." Camila smirks.

My blood boils. Eleni isn't some *thing* Camila can come here and make snide comments about.

"She is my girlfriend and—" I barely catch myself from blurting the words "mother of my children." We haven't even begun to broach that topic yet. I simply glare at Camila.

She puts her hands up. "No offense meant. Really, I should've known. You're approaching that age."

"The age where men marry strippers they've known for seventy-two hours?" I ask, deadpan.

Her smirk barely flickers, unhurt by the jab. Her relationship with her husband was an open secret.

I point to the door. "I take care of you because my code dictates that I do, as a widow of my organization. Reducing that care would be no great burden." I look her up and down. "I strongly doubt anyone would object if I threw you out on your gold-digging ass."

She sniffs and strides out without another word. I drop into the seat behind my desk and put my head in my hands. Fucking Camila. How long has it been since we even talked? She always had big ideas about what belongs to her, even back when Marco was one of my dad's senior capos. I've never put much stock in the rumor she killed him, but I couldn't deny she was better without him. Bigger. Even when bigger was fucking annoying like this.

My phone rings, and I check the caller ID. My heart skips a beat. I pick up.

"I figured you'd call eventually. Is this line tapped, or can we talk like men?"

3 2

NORMAL GIRL

Eleni

"Wait, there's seriously a ceremony?" I ask as I pick through a wooden tray of pears for the best ones.

Seb glances at the stall owner. "Yes. Do you know you talk very loud?"

I roll my eyes and pay for the three pears. "We're in the middle of one of the busiest farmer's markets in Brooklyn on a Saturday afternoon. I'd discuss the nuclear codes here if I had them. Now tell me, what exactly does the ceremony for becoming a capo entail? I skipped that step."

He laughs and accepts the bag I hand him. This has become something of a routine for us. Dante said being a boss, even a part-time one, means having at least one bodyguard at all times, and Seb was an easy pick. He's actually fun to talk to and hangs out instead of hovering three feet behind me at all times.

"It's not like a graduation ceremony, if that's what you're picturing."

"I was picturing something much more Arthurian," I say. "Like Dante with a big sword, knighting you."

He shakes his head. "Try again."

"It's a big gun!" I giggle. "Or, no, it's like one of those cult things where you all have to wear velvet robes and chant in Latin!"

He laughs along with me. "You couldn't be farther, but since you're being such a dick, I won't tell you."

"No!" I loop my arm through his and bat my eyelashes. "I super, totally want to know."

"Okay." He lowers his voice and leans in conspiratorially. "There's a reason the ceremony only happens at the end of the summer. It's because secretly we all get naked and sit in a pool full of special moonlight that gives us wolf powers." He throws his head back and howls.

People turn to look at us. I smack his arm and try not to totally dissolve in laughter. Another key element of our errand runs? Both of us are trying to out-embarrass the other by making a bigger scene. I've never had a younger brother, but I dreamed about it all the time when I was a kid. Talking with Seb feels almost exactly like that. Like hanging out with Christos, except Seb's not trying to be smarter all the time. It's just so easy.

I hip-check him while he checks out a girl's ass, and he stumbles. "You'll tell me for real sometime, right?"

"Nah, at this point I think it's more fun if it's a surprise." He laughs. "You'll just have to show up and see."

His genuine excitement shines through his every pore. I can't help remembering when he first admitted he wanted to be a capo in the woods behind the safe house. He got his dream so quickly. Now, to get mine, all I have to do is graduate from one of the most prestigious engineering colleges in New York. While holding down my position in the Saints.

For a second, I wish I'm a normal girl, out on a Saturday with her brother. The pieces snap into place. I'm an average college student who got an exciting opportunity, and he just got a promotion at his dream job. I have this guy I think I'm excited about, and he's a chronic bachelor. In my mind's eye, Dante transforms into a severe CEO with nothing more illegitimate than a few accidental insider trades on his record. Now that I'm not chasing revenge and the syndicate doesn't need me at its head, it's much easier to imagine a life without it.

"Earth to Eleni." Seb snaps his fingers in front of my eyes.

I blink and return to reality. "Sorry."

Someone slams into my shoulder, and I drop the bag of produce I'm holding. A burst of real pain spirals out of the impact point, and anger surges through me.

"Who the hell do you think—" I look up, up, up at the man who smashed into me. A real mountain of flesh, large in every dimension, and those dimensions are unmistakably filled with muscle. I swallow, and my hand twitches for the gun I still carry in my waistband.

He sneers at me and starts to walk away.

Seb steps into his path. "You gonna fucking apologize?"

The massive man snorts and tries to walk around Seb.

"No, you just hit a woman." Seb dodges back and forth to block his way. "Were you raised in a goddamn barn?"

I want to tell Seb to leave it be, but I know how this works now. The man could just be an asshole, but if he belongs to another syndicate, Seb needs to show them I'm not alone out here. I slide my hand under my shirt and caress the butt of my gun, hoping against hope I don't have to pull it in the middle of this crowded space. Maybe if I got in tight, I could press it to the bastard's side, make him leave without a fuss.

The first guy shoves Seb, exposing the black-and-white tattoo that covers most of the man's arm. I think I recognize it, but it disappears too quickly for me to be certain.

Seb stumbles back a step. "So, it's like that?"

He swings a punch at the taller man's face. The man catches his fist and just stares at it. I study the tattoo in more detail. It's a building with multiple towers. Fuck, I learned so many different signs and symbols when I was trying to get a hold on New York's organized crime. Why can't I place this one?

Seb hisses in pain, and I realize the man is trying to crush his fist.

Two more men, almost as large as the first, flank the man Seb is antagonizing. I catch the split-second downturn of his mouth, a tell he no longer likes his odds. My move.

I shove myself in between Seb and the men, then with a pounding heart put my back to them and my hands on my hips. "I want to go. There's a sale downtown, and I'm not missing it for your macho bullshit."

The men snicker.

"You hear the little lady," one of them says in a thick accent. "We will let you go."

As the men turn to leave, the accent and the tattoo click. That was a Russian church, with four towers for four prison sentences served. In Russia.

My skin goes cold with the reminder I'm very much not a normal girl anymore.

33

SPOILED

Dante

I WALK into my house after another long day at Piacere trying to figure out if Cal Duncan's information is worth anything, and I have nothing on my mind but a quiet night at home with El. The empty foyer echoes with my footsteps, but she's been working on getting ready for school in her office upstairs, so I trudge up.

At the top of the stairs, the door to Eleni's office stands closed, but my—our?—bedroom door is open, and light spills out onto the floor. I frown and walk in.

"Dante!" Eleni leans out of the bathroom. A few perfect curls swing away from her updo, and a long, silver earring that kind of looks like an elegant stick jingles. "You're earlier than I thought."

"Sorry?" I step farther into the room and realize she's just wearing a towel. "Did I forget we had plans?"

She laughs. "It's a surprise."

I nod slowly, trying to put together the clues. Fancy hair. Two garment bags sit on the bed. She's smiling.

"Yeah, I got nothing," I say.

She steps out of the bathroom and kisses me softly. "Between eating with you every night and the reports I'm getting from my guys, it's no secret you're stressed."

I run a hand over my hair. "I'm just tired. There's nothing—"

She silences me with another kiss. "We have reservations at a Michelin star restaurant in the city in an hour. Get dressed, or I'll leave without you." She grabs one of the garment bags off the bed and saunters back into the bathroom, then kicks the door closed.

Warmth pours through my chest. She realized I was stressed and planned something to relax me. I open the other garment bag and change into the slim cut, deep red suit—with matching deep red tie and shirt, I note with a smile—then sit back on the bed to wait for Eleni. I don't just have to come home to an empty house and keep thinking about work all night anymore. Fuck, I could even pick her brain about this. I'm so goddamn stupid not to have done this already.

The bathroom door opens. She wears a long, slinky black gown with a tantalizingly high slit. I swallow and decide to act the gentleman, at least until her surprise is over. I want to let her take care of me. What a strange impulse. I stand and offer her my arm.

She takes it. "Armando is driving us into the city, and we have a room walking distance from the restaurant."

I grin. "You're going to spoil me if you're not careful."

She laughs. "I'd like to see that."

THE RESTAURANT TURNS out to be a seafood place in upper Manhattan I've been meaning to try for ages. I smile as we enter.

"Did someone tell you about this?"

"They didn't have to." She kisses my cheek. "You had it bookmarked on your laptop."

I laugh. "Did you find that before or after you moved all of my shit around?"

The hostess shoots me a look, and I duck my head apologetically. One of the reasons I've never been is because I heard a rumor there was a strict code of conduct. But if there's one thing Eleni and I can both enjoy, it's breaking the rules. She giggles behind her hand as the stern hostess leads us to a corner table, notably away from most of the other guests, and informs us frostily that our waiter will be by for drink orders soon.

"Why did you move all my shit around?" I ask a little quieter. "I liked it where it was."

She rolls her eyes. "Because the only thing you had protecting your shit was a geriatric antivirus I made Mama and Baba stop using years ago. Half the beat cops in this city could've broken in."

I shake my head, trying to fight off reminders of work. "I had a password."

She levels a glare at me. "The password was your dad's birthday. I guessed it on the second try."

I scowl down at my menu as the waiter walks up. It couldn't have been that bad, could it? I ran the Saints for years without El and without issue. I order a top-shelf scotch. Eleni considers for a moment, then asks for something called "Charisma." The waiter nods like that makes any sense and leaves.

"What the hell did you just do?" I ask to try to distract myself from the issue of cybersecurity. She's spoiling me tonight. My job is to enjoy that.

"It's a cocktail." She shows me with a smile.

The listing on the menu describes something frothy and tropical, with more different alcohols than almost anything else. I raise an eyebrow.

"I'm still experimenting." She shrugs, a little embarrassed. "I had my first real drink in Piacere, the night of the auction."

The memory of her coughing brings a smile to my lips, but the mention of Piacere just reminds me of all the work waiting for me on the other side of this date. My hands twitches for my phone. If I text Tony now, he can—

El holds her hand out. "Phone."

"What?"

"Give me your phone." She wiggles her fingers. "You're distracted, and I'd love to know why, but I'm not going to ask while you can 'just give Tony a quick call,' you know?"

Emotions war in my chest. There's something intoxicating about being known so well, and something deeply embarrassing about having my flaws laid out in front of me. Especially when I know she's right.

"Fuck it." I slap my phone in her palm. "They'll probably call you if anything goes sideways."

She smiles and sets it on the edge of the table. "Now tell me. I know there's something new."

"Cal Duncan called Tony and I for a meeting."

The waiter drops off our drinks and asks if we're ready to order. Eleni answers before I can, informing him we'll be having the tasting menu for two. I smile at her confidence. She looks almost nothing like the woman I met in the Greek Corner, but I can see a little of her in that smile, in the way she talks to the staff. I remain silent until he's gone, then lean in and drop my voice low.

"The short version is, he says there's a mole in the Saints."

Eleni's eyebrows shoot up. "Does he know who?"

I shrug. "Someone I knew as a kid got out of the life and went federal. He's the one sniffing around, but I don't know who his moles might be."

She nods. "What can we do?"

The "we" hums through me like I'm a tuning fork. I grin despite the topic. "Weed them out. It takes fucking forever, and there's no relaxing until it's done, though."

Her gaze goes thoughtful. "How do you usually do that?"

"We create a short list. New guys, guys who have been shady, anyone we think is worth checking out," I say. "Then, we drop different scraps of fake information, and wait to see which of them turns into a raid. Whoever we gave that, we take out."

The waiter arrives, and the first course disappears under conversation about logistics of spreading the information, different pieces of the process we could automate. She lights up with focus, and suddenly, talking about work doesn't feel like an endless slog. My world expands in her eyes.

The second course appears, and she picks up her fork, then looks at me. "You said this was federal? How worried should we be?"

I shake my head. "Feds are tough, but the truth is, it's pretty tough to build a case against me unless they find me with a hot gun in my hand. Plus, half the NYPD is on my payroll, and I'm the biggest donor to the precincts on Staten Island every year."

"So you don't think we have to worry at all." She takes a bite of the food and moans softly.

The sound travels through me like I'm a live wire, and my cock springs to attention.

"Not yet," I say roughly. "So what do you say we talk about something other than work?"

Eleni looks me over with a small smile and nods.

3 4

GIVE AND TAKE

Eleni

I TAKE one last bite of the airy sorbet that the stuffy waiter brought for dessert and look at Dante. He's barely glanced away from me since we stopped talking about work, and my body burns with it. I slide my leg out from under the long tablecloth, letting it catch my skirt and exposing inch after inch of skin. He watches me with darkening eyes.

"Put that away," he says.

I smile. "Why?"

"Because I don't share well."

I tuck my leg back under the table. Seeing him relax after days of walking around in a fog is satisfying, though, and I'm not sure I want to give everything up yet. I toe out of one heel and run my foot up the inside of his calf.

"How sure are you that you can wait?" I ask.

He grasps the edge of the table. "What are you doing?

I chuckle and keep running my foot smoothly up and down. "That's not an order."

He meets my gaze. "Don't expose yourself here, pet."

My skin goes hot. We've never played like this in public before. I don't even know if he sees the loophole he's left me.

"Yes, sir." I caress the curve of his knee. His knuckles start to turn white, but he doesn't stop me. I slouch a little in my chair so I can reach his inner thigh. His gaze flickers down to my chest, my breasts pressed higher by my position.

"Careful," he warns through gritted teeth.

I smile and ghost my foot over his crotch. As I expected, he's already hard.

"Can you call for the check, sir? I doubt we're going to want to stay much longer."

His answering smile is hungry. He raises his hand, and I wait until the waiter turns away to get it. Then, I duck under the table.

"Pet," Dante says sharply.

I unfasten his belt. "I'm not exposed, sir."

He hisses out a breath as I free his cock. No time to waste. The waiter has been fast all night. I lick my lips and take Dante in my mouth. Silverware clatters, and he curses under his breath. I grin. He grows to his full length in my mouth, presses against the back of my throat already. I blink back stinging tears and ease forward. Dante snakes one hand under the table and grabs hold of my hair. I track his reactions in the minute tightening and loosening of his fingers, coaxing him to the edge of climax as quickly as I can.

"Your check, sir," the waiter says.

Dante clenches down on my hair, trying to drag me to a stop. But that's not his safe word. I grin at the pain and move faster.

"Thank you." He sounds choked. "Ah, are you going to wait while I—?"

"That's protocol, sir," he says. "Will you and madam need any boxes tonight? Is she in the bathroom?"

The head of Dante's cock slides down my throat. I moan as quietly as I can, teasing him with the vibrations. His hand in my hair becomes a brilliant spot of pain, leaving me panting.

"No," he says tightly. "Thank you."

Dante's hips jerk against my mouth. He's so close I can taste it in slim, salty ribbons.

"Have a good night, sir," the waiter says.

A beat of silence passes. Dante slams himself down my mouth and spills. I catch every drop, swallowing as fast as I can, then duck out from under the table.

"I'm back from the bathroom, sir." I smile sweetly. "Should we go?"

<hr>

DANTE REMAINS silent until we step into the empty elevator on the way up to our hotel room. Want curls in my gut, but nervous anticipation jangles my limbs. I know his thinking face.

"You're pleased with yourself for that little loophole, aren't you, pet?" he asks quietly.

I swallow. "Yes, sir."

He nods. "You didn't disobey. But you tempted me to break my own rules."

I meet his gaze in the reflective elevator doors. "How, sir?"

He grabs my chin and forces me to face him. "Do you have any idea how hard it was not to drag you out from under that table, bend you over it, and fuck you where the whole restaurant could see? Declare to them that you're all fucking mine?"

I shake my head as the picture he paints courses through me in a wave of desire.

"Of course you don't." He slaps me lightly. "Someone has to keep their head. Just know, pet, every little loophole you escape through will close on you eventually."

I shudder, and he wraps his arm around my waist with a grip like iron. Silence chases us through the rest of the ride and down the hallway to our door. I pause in the entryway.

"Am I permitted clothes, sir?"

Dante lets go of me and waltzes in. I glance both ways down the hall. Empty. I slide off the dress, then the matching bra and panties I picked out to go with it, and bring everything inside. He's already disappeared into the bedroom, throwing golden light through the dark suite. I shut the door and hurry after him.

He stands over the box of toys I ordered here, just in case, picking through them lazily.

"You're getting bossy," he says as I enter.

I duck my head. "Sorry, sir."

"Bed," he replies. "Touch yourself. I want to watch."

I know myself much better than I did the first time I received this instruction. I drop onto the bed and slide my fingers through my soaking folds, then circle my clit slowly.

"Faster," he barks.

My fingers race, playing my body like an instrument. I moan.

"Good." He rakes his gaze over me. "I'm going to shower. Come twice before I return." He meets my eyes. "Don't lie, pet."

I nod, and he walks away. Twice. He showers so fast. Luckily, my body is already electric after my performance in the restaurant. The water turns on. He didn't shut the door. I let noises slip from my lips, a testament to my hard work. My first orgasm comes quickly, shaking and crying out his name. I breathe a few times, then return my hand between my legs to try again. The second wave of pleasure builds. I'm paying for what I've done. Dante is going to come back and tell me my fate. I don't want to disappoint—

The water shuts off. A desperate cry escapes my mouth, but I haven't come yet. Maybe he'll get dressed, take his time.

He steps out of the bathroom seconds later in a towel and looks me over. "How many?"

"One," I nearly sob.

He clicks his tongue. The burning disapproval in his gaze is enough to send me careening over the edge in anticipation.

"Too little, too late." Dante sighs. "Two more, while I watch, or I won't touch you."

"Two more?" I study him for any sign of mercy.

He backhands me lazily. "You're lucky I'm letting you try again at all."

"Of course." My hands shakes as I drag it back between my shining thighs.

"Spread your legs."

I obey.

"Touch your tits."

I bring my other hand to my breasts and tease my nipples to peaks. His critical, incisive gaze makes the third orgasm easy. Pleasure sparkles through my vision, hot and sharp-edged. I relax onto the bed.

"Another," he barks.

Overwhelmed tears trail down my cheeks, but I don't even consider using my safe word. I've earned this. Something rustles, and I open my eyes. Dante has shed the towel, and he's touching himself lazily. I moan at the sight.

"Please," I beg. "I learned my lesson. Please fuck me."

He smiles. "You beg prettily. But you haven't learned shit. Come for me."

I sink my teeth into my lower lip and throw everything I have into touching myself. I scrape my free hand over my breasts, my neck, my sides, my hair, anything that might push me over the edge. A fourth orgasm teeters on the edge of my vision. Overstimulation threatens.

"I can't do it without you," I sob.

"There it is." Dante's on me in a second, and I don't know when he put a condom on, but I feel the familiar slide of latex as he thrusts inside.

I fling my arms around his next and hold on, weeping with pleasure. He sets an unforgiving pace and plucks at my nipples, summoning sparks of pain. I careen over the edge moments later with a scream, and he keeps fucking me. A fifth orgasm, so pleasurable it borders on pain, sears through me before he stiffens and comes, hissing the word, "Mine."

I laugh breathlessly as the sixth orgasm tears up my limbs.

3 5

AFTERCARE

Eleni

THE RISING sun peeks through the heavy hotel curtain as I lean back into Dante's hands in the massive bathtub. He smooths conditioner over my hair, the final step in our now usual aftercare routine. I sigh and continue picking up the pieces of myself that scatter when he takes me apart like that. Still, I always return to myself looser-limbed and more at ease than before.

Dante drops a kiss on my soapy shoulder. "How are you doing, El?"

"Good." I smile. "You?"

He chuckles. "Grateful that little stunt didn't get us kicked out of the restaurant. I liked the food."

I grin. "And the blowjob?'

"Now I know you're back." He shakes his head. "The blowjob, I can get at home. Or anywhere else, it seems."

I stretch out as I laugh. Through the soapy water, I can just see my tanned legs next to Dante's longer, paler ones. I tangle my ankle with his just to feel him in more places.

"Do you ever daydream about that?" I ask.

169

Dante removes his hands from my hair. "Don't rinse yet, it needs to sit. Daydream about your mouth? Daily."

I giggle. "That's not what I meant, but I don't believe you."

He wraps one arm around my waist, heavy and warmer than the cooling water. I snuggle in.

"El, you've got a mouth men could write poetry about." He kisses my cheek. "Daily might be undershooting."

Sleep starts to wind greedy fingers into my muscles. As soon as we leave the bath, I'm going to pass out. But I need to stay awake a little longer.

"Having sex in other places," I say.

He hums. "I assume you want something more specific than I haven't entered a space in the last three months without thinking about fucking you there?"

I nod as embers of arousal warm in my core. It's too late—and I'm too sore—to do anything else, but I enjoy the feeling anyway.

"Piacere, certainly," he says. "In a few different places. The middle of the dance floor. My office, properly this time. The room where we met."

I grin. "Playing out the fantasy of taking me up on my initial offer?"

He nods with a sly smile.

"We could do that, if you weren't so goddamn busy," I mumble.

"You've been busy too," he answers mildly. "I got home early on Saturday, and you were out with Seb for another two hours."

"Saturday?" The back of my mind, like I've forgotten something important.

"You came home with all that produce?" He curls some of my hair around one of his fingers.

"Oh!" I sit up, though I instantly miss his warmth against my back. "Some Russian slammed into me. I completely forgot to tell you."

He chuckles and pulls me back. "Seb didn't forget."

"He told you about the tattoos?" I frown. "And how fucking big they were?"

"The second part took a little more convincing, but yes." Dante kisses along the line of my neck. "Why do you bring this up now?"

"Because...." I shake my head, struggling to keep my thoughts in order when I know sleep is so close. "Because I couldn't find anything about them while you were healing other than rumors."

"They're very secretive," Dante says.

"I don't even know who their fucking boss is," I complain.

He laughs. "Neither do I, but I've got men on it. I don't think a couple Russians in a market are anything to worry about, though."

His voice is so soft, so smooth. Dante knows what he's talking about. He wouldn't lie to me, and he wouldn't put me in danger if he didn't have to. I nod.

"Let's get you in bed before you fall asleep," he says. "Rinse."

I'm not inclined to disagree with much of anything anymore. I wash the conditioner off underwater, then surface. Dante stands first, and I twist to watch the water sheet off his bare body. A cluster of bubbles clings to his hip bone, and I swipe it away with a finger. He smiles softly down at me, then steps out. I lean against the side of the tub, my eyelids drooping, as he wraps himself in one plush, cream-colored hotel towel and throws a second one over his shoulder.

He returns to me and holds out his hands. "Time to get up."

I grumble, but I like this part almost as much as all of the others. Dante's hands are strong and muscular in mine as he helps me stand, but all of the threat of that strength has drained away. The arm that catches me when I stumble stepping over the high wall holds nothing but promise and protection. He wraps the second hotel towel around me, and the soft fabric soothes the new bruises on my skin. Dimly, my mind drifts to the ring box. He hasn't said a word about that yet. If I were him, and I was going to...I don't know, propose, I'd pick a moment like this.

Dante lifts me to sit on the counter and drags a wide-toothed comb coated in thick moisturizer through my hair, section by section.

The first time he tried this aftercare routine and let me go to sleep right after the bath like I wanted to, I woke up with my hair in such a snarl that I think I would've gotten it all cut off if we hadn't been at the safe house upstate at the time.

After that, he made me walk him through what I did with my hair after a shower and memorized every step. I stare up at him as he tends to me. His dark eyes are soft, and the small tension furrow between his brows only appears when he hits a few particularly tangled curls. He hums to himself softly as he works, but I've never asked him what song it is. By this point, I can rarely muster the energy to speak. I love the song, though. I love Dante.

He lifts me in his arms and carries me to the bed. I pull off the towel and tuck myself under the covers while he circles around and joins me on the opposite side. As soon as he lays down, I pillow my head on his chest. He wraps an arm around me and doesn't say a word. The ring box appears in my mind again. I'd definitely choose a moment like this. So if he isn't, maybe I'm wrong. I never opened the box. It could be any—

I fall asleep before I finish the thought.

SIZING UP

Eleni

A FEW WEEKS after the hotel date, I look over the table of classes on my laptop one last time and shut it with a smile. My first registration at Tandon, and I got all the classes I wanted! I text Dante about my success and laugh when he responds with a huge thumbs-up. He texts like he protects his data, but I've grown used to the labyrinth of old-timey habits and emoji usages. He's thrilled. And, with any luck, bored out of his mind at Piacere.

He put out the hooks for potential rats to snap up a little while ago, and nothing has caught yet. That means a full day of sitting around waiting for disaster, which makes him feel, in his words, "like a fireman without a fire," so he's been coming home a little grumpy, but watching his mood improve as soon as he sees me makes it really easy not to take personally.

Plus, we're now going on—I check the date—just about two and a half weeks without any deaths in the organization. The quiet made getting ready for school a lot easier. Dante even found time for a drive upstate to visit Christos' grave. I cleaned it sparkling and cried, but that chapter finally feels settled. Now, I just have to make it through the last month before classes actually start.

The door opens downstairs, and I hop up.

"Be right down!" I call.

"Hurry up!" Gianna yells back. "You know all the good tables disappear if we arrive at like, 9:01."

I trade my sweatpants for a pair of loose, blue floral shorts and pull a fitted, silky, navy crop top over my casual sports bra. A sheer, lacy version of the long blazer Gianna suggested completes the look, and I race downstairs, throwing my hair up in a bun as I go.

Gianna looks like she's about to walk some kind of brunch-based runway in a pink dress that clings and drapes like lingerie. "You look cute, I love you, I'm going to kill you if we don't leave. These reservations are *impossible* to get."

I laugh. "Go, go!"

She races out the still-open door, and I snag a pair of cork platforms before following barefoot in case she decides to leave without me.

Finally, we arrive at what Gianna deemed the best upscale brunch spot in Manhattan and are seated with what I've figured out is pretty much minimum eye-rolling from a hostess working the brunch shift in Manhattan. Gianna drops into her neon-yellow metal chair with a sigh.

"Sorry," she says. "You really do look cute."

I shake my head as I sit. "It's fine. I was just finishing up registration and didn't have time to change."

Gianna drops her head onto the table and covers it with her arms. "Oh my god, I'm such a bitch. I completely forgot." She peeks up at me through a gap. "How did it go?"

"Good!" I laugh as I pick up a menu. "I got everything I wanted. A full schedule, which is kind of intimidating."

An eye-rolling waitress appears, and Gianna sits up instantly, then relaxes into what she calls her "cool girl slouch." I hide a smile. In Piacere, on most of Staten Island, she walks around like she runs the place. The city, I've realized, is a different ball game for her. One where I actually have the experience to give me an advantage, not that I ever ate breakfast this expensive before the Saints. I just know nobody in New York City actually gives a shit what anybody else is doing.

While Gianna preens, I manage to order bottomless mimosas for both of us and a Greek-inspired omelet for myself. She remembers to get a bacon, egg, and cheese sandwich at the last second.

"If anybody can handle school and this life, it's you," she says when the waitress leaves. "I'm pretty sure you're the smartest person I've ever met."

"You're just—"

"Gianna? Eleni?" someone says behind me.

I turn to see Camila standing from another table in the restaurant to display a clinging sundress the color of old lace.

"I thought it was you." She walks over with a wide smile. "Is it your first time? I absolutely love this place. I would have brought you if I'd known you were interested."

"It is," Gianna says a little tightly. "And that's so sweet, but I don't know when you would've had time in your busy schedule."

Camila laughs the sort of laugh you usually hear from princesses in movies. "My schedule? I'd be worried about yours. You're still working at Piacere, aren't you?"

I glance at Gianna as her jaw tightens.

"I am," she says. "But that leaves my days pretty free. I have a firm policy about leaving work at work instead of taking it home."

My gaze bounces back to Camila like I'm watching a tennis match.

"To each their own, I suppose. I've found a lot of success in going after what I want rather than waiting for it to come to me." Camila turns to me with a megawatt smile. "Eleni, right? I saw you from across the barbecue but didn't get a chance to introduce myself."

She was at the barbecue for almost three hours, but if Gianna's strained politeness is anything to go by, now isn't the time to bring that up. I stick out a hand to shake.

"Eleni Calimeris."

She giggles like shaking hands is the funniest thing in the world, but accepts my offer to shake. "Camila Donato. Pleasure to make your acquaintance."

Her hand is soft, like she's never done any work, but there's a strength in her grip I can't deny. She's the one who pumps up, then down, and releases.

"How did you end up at the barbecue?" I ask. "I hadn't heard of you before then, and I ran the Saints for a couple weeks."

Her pale eyebrows shoot up in what looks like fake surprise. "Ran it? I'm surprised Dante could give up control for that long."

I straighten. "He needed someone. I stepped up."

She hums, dragging her gaze up and down my outfit. "Well, who among us doesn't know what it's like to be needed by Dante Cattaneo?"

Her gaze cuts through me like a knife, searching for weaknesses. My stomach drops to my toes. Does she mean...?

Distantly, I hear Gianna say, "Um, me. Can we help you with something?"

"Just saying hello." Camila flutters a playful wave. "I'll return to my breakfast now."

She waltzes away as the first round of our bottomless mimosas arrive. I grab mine, down it in a few gulps, and put the glass back on the waitress' tray for a refill. Dante slept with her. Or she slept with Dante. There's no other way to interpret that.

Gianna takes one sip and raises an eyebrow. "All good?"

"Why do you hate her?" I demand.

She coughs. "I don't *hate* Camila. I just...." She shakes her head. "I don't know, I don't usually listen to the wives' gossip, but have you noticed how she basically only wears white?"

I nod. It's like she thinks she's in a movie or showing off that she's too perfect to ever spill.

"Well, she wore white to her husband's funeral. Claimed it was a mourning thing in her family." Gianna looks over my shoulder and narrows her eyes. "But years later? After she's scorched her way through the socialite circuit? I've barely had a conversation with the woman, but let's just say I wouldn't have a hard time believing she offed him."

My blood boils. I accept my second mimosa and focus on staying sober enough to confront Dante as soon as we get out of here. He lied to me.

3 7

PANTS ON FIRE

Eleni

GIANNA—WHOM I now hate—picks up on my bitchy mood after our run-in with Camila and not only makes me stay at brunch long enough to sober up but comes home with me and hangs out for the rest of the day, inventing new activities every time I get bored enough to get pissed about Camila all over again.

My phone vibrates on the edge of the bathtub next to me. I glance at it. A text from Dante, letting me know he's on his way home. I lift it and silently show the screen to Gianna.

"Perfect." She caps the bright-blue nail polish bottle in her hands. "I just finished."

I wiggle my neon-painted toes. "You know you didn't have to stick around all day, right?"

She shakes her head and stands. "You'd think you never had a best friend before."

"I haven't," I admit.

She takes my hand, the expression on her face softening. "Fuck, I didn't realize."

179

I shrug. "It's not a big deal, really. I had friends. I was just too busy with The Greek Corner to ever become anybody's go-to."

"It absolutely is a big deal, and if I let this summer end without a sleepover, you have full permission to shoot me." She grins and releases my hand to pack up our makeshift beauty day. "For the uninitiated, one of the primary jobs of a best friend is to keep her best friend from doing something stupid because she's mad and/or drunk." She laughs. "Or both."

My face warms. "Sorry. But you think this is stupid? I'm freaking out over nothing?"

"I think you should talk to him without your other best friend, Miss Champagne, running the show." She squeezes my shoulder. "I'm out before Dante shows. I love you both, but I'm not getting caught in the middle."

She breezes out, and a few moments later, I hear the door open and shut. I'm definitely less furious than I was earlier. And way less drunk, despite the headachy reminder. I head downstairs to make a pot of coffee and wait for Dante.

He arrives just as I'm pouring myself a cup. "El?"

"In here," I call. "Coffee?"

He rounds into the kitchen. "Please. I've had a hell of a day."

Dante kisses the side of my head as I pour him a second mug, and a little of my earlier anger reignites.

"How was your day?" he asks.

A little sears into way too much.

"You slept with Camila," I blurt.

He sets down his cup and blows out a long breath. "So you went into the city."

"You're not denying it." I cross my arms, the headache pounding in my temples.

"No, I'm not." He looks at me. "I slept with Camila. Several times."

My chest aches. I start to turn away. Fuck, I'm so stupid.

He catches my arm. "Way before I met you. El, did she say something?"

I whip back. "I fucking hope it was before I met you! Why didn't you tell me when I asked?"

He winces. "So that's the actual problem. Great."

"Don't say 'great' like that." I pull out of his grasp. "All resigned, like you already know how this is going to end."

"I do know." He offers me a soft smile. "Because I'm very, very sorry for not telling you, and the fact that I didn't go into detail about my prior relationship with her after she showed up at the barbecue."

I search his gaze. He looks honest. But he looked honest when he was lying to me a lot.

"Prove it," I say. "Explain. Why didn't you tell me?"

He scrubs a hand through his hair and loosens his tie. "Because it's kind of embarrassing."

I roll my eyes. "Oh, yeah, and I never told you about that torrid summer I spent getting passed around by international supermodels because they'd really hurt my reputation."

"Are you going to let me finish a goddamn thought, or should I order you a Dante cutout to yell at until you're ready to talk?" he snaps.

I sarcastically mime locking my lips.

"Camila's one of those women who always has a different mafia guy on her arm." He shakes his head. "She's beautiful, she's fun, but you get involved knowing it's never going to be for long, and knowing everyone else is thinking the same goddamn thing. Once I took over the Saints, I suddenly found her in my lap at every party until I gave in." He clears his throat.

Beautiful. Fun. Why the hell was he embarrassed?

"She took that a little more personally. Started getting jealous when I saw other women, demanding more time with me." He shakes his head. "I didn't have time for anything serious, and even if I did, I wouldn't have pursued it with her. Cam's all surface-level sparkle."

Cam. I want to melt into a puddle. Dante stares at me for a long moment.

"You can talk now," he says testily.

I mime unlocking my lips for a second to gather my thoughts. "How long?"

"What?"

"How long did she"—I swallow—"*sparkle* for?"

He grimaces. "A little less than a year."

I turn to leave again. A year. He refused to tell me about a year-long relationship because of internal mafia politics I had no way of knowing. I need to go.

"Please, El," he says. "You have to believe me. Cam was...not a mistake, but a blip on the radar. It's embarrassing for a boss to fall for someone like her, and I forgot you didn't know that."

I look at him with tears in my eyes. "Fall for?"

He sighs and pulls me into a hug. "Fall for her tricks. As you seem to have. Trust me, I know the mark they leave."

Dante holds me tight, and I breathe in the idea that he was protecting his reputation. That he cares about what I think. That he's worried about what Camila might've done to me. I wrap my arms around his waist.

"Sorry," I mutter against his suit. "Gianna told me not to freak, but I asked you, and you lied, so...."

He kisses the top of my head. "So I looked like a monster. I get it. But you'll tell me if she tries to mess with you again? I haven't had a public girlfriend since we broke it off, and she might be getting territorial."

I nod. "Just...nothing's happening between you now, right?"

"It's been years," he says easily. "Now please, forget about her. I had a shitty day, but I have a surprise for you."

I lean back from his chest and eye him. "What kind of surprise?"

"So suspicious!" He laughs. "The kind you have to wait for tomorrow morning to receive."

I shove him playfully. "Then how is that a surprise tonight?"

He shrugs with a smirk, and I decide to put the Camila thing out of my mind. He's telling the truth. She does seem like the jealous type. But as Dante wanders off to grab takeout menus and discuss dinner, my mind drifts to the ring box. That couldn't be the surprise, could it?

3 8

RAT TRAIL

Dante

I ADJUST my tie in the pale moonlight slanting in through the window and glance at Eleni over my shoulder. She's sprawled across the bed, as always, with her hair everywhere. I pull my attention back and tighten it a little more. Sneaking out of bed in the middle of the night like this feels oddly like a betrayal after the fight this afternoon, but it's not as though I'm going to see Camila. And, truth told, I'll do just about anything to keep as much space between Cal Duncan and Eleni as possible. I pat the gun already holstered on my hip and creep out of the room.

Tony waits for me in a car outside, not idling in case that draws the attention of the neighbors. They tend to have their ears a little extra pricked in the weeks after the barbecue. All the accountants and lawyers around here aren't exactly subtle about wanting an invite, but I don't think they'd blend with the crowd. I slide into the passenger's seat, and Tony turns on the car.

"It's my job as your caporegime to say Cal Duncan might be luring us to a trap in the middle of the night," he says.

"And it's my duty as the boss to do this." I wait until he brakes at a stop sign, then thump the back of his head. "I fucking know that."

Tony snorts. "Right. And that's why you haven't breathed a word to a fucking soul about the fact that we're doing this."

"You don't know that." I stare out the window as he leaves the gated neighborhood and heads for the Verrazano.

"The only reason you'd make me wait outside like a boyfriend you don't want your parents to meet is if Eleni was asleep when you left." He glances at me. "Which means you didn't tell her."

"Next time I get to pick my caporegime, I'm choosing someone less nosy," I grumble. "He set the fucking meeting, anyway, and it's your little brother we're looking into the Russians about."

"Seb stumbled into them first, but he didn't start this." Tony shakes his head. "And fuck me, I believe Cal Duncan's scared of the Russians."

I nod, thinking back on the phone call I received after Camila left the other day. Cal had been his usual, overdramatic self, but when I tried to tell him again I had no interest in working together, he'd been very insistent this would benefit us both. Only when he mentioned a potential Russian hideout in the city had I changed my tune. "Accidentally" running into Seb and El was one thing. Setting up shop is another entirely, and I intend to put out whatever fire they intended to start before it blazed out of control. Even if that means working with Cal fucking Duncan.

Tony lets the subject drop, and we drive the rest of the way to the meatpacking district in silence. My thoughts race. Part of me is glad to be prowling the streets in the dead of night. It isn't like I'd be sleeping, with my plans for tomorrow. We pull up to the appointed corner and find Cal standing in the halogen glow of a streetlight. Tony parks, and we climb out.

"Evening, gentlemen," Cal says as we walk up. "I was starting to think you were going to miss our date."

"Stow the attitude, Duncan," I reply. "You said you had something worth dragging my ass out of bed in the middle of the night for. What is it?"

"Now, is that any way to talk to a man just trying to be your friend?" His smile highlights his spattering of freckles. "I notice that while I abided by our agreement to do this as equals, you've brought muscle."

Tony pushes hair out of his ice-blue eyes in the way I know he practices to make his arms seem bigger. Douche. Thank god he's here.

I turn back to Cal. "We're a package deal. Feel free to bring your second next time."

The implication lingers between us. I'm open to a next time. And I'm not scared of whatever he thinks he has up his sleeve.

"Much appreciated." He inclines his head. "Walk with me."

He strides away. Tony rolls his eyes at me. I shrug in agreement and follow the Irish bastard.

"I've a friend I call Russ," Cal says conversationally. "His family's Irish by way of Slovakia, but the difference is lost on most of my men, so they called him 'the Russian' for ages. Does a grand Russian accent, besides."

I stuff my hands in my pockets and try not to look pissed at his meandering story. Tony is doing a shittier job than me, at least.

"When you toppled the Lombardis, there was a bit of a vacuum." Cal leads us into a crappy apartment building. "Your girl did an admirable job stepping up, but the territory was already shaky with Frank gone. So the damned Russians started poking."

"Do you have a friend called 'the point' as well?" Tony asks.

Cal smirks at him as he steps up to the deathtrap of an elevator. "Just waiting for a bit of clean air."

The elevator opens immediately, and I eye the tiny box, then all of us.

"We're not—"

"Alas, we are." Cal grins. "It's this or thirty flights of stairs, and I didn't pack my running shoes."

Tony and I exchange another look, then step in shoulder-to-shoulder. Cal fucking Duncan. If anything's going to be a trap tonight, it's this. Despite the squeeze, I work my hand onto the grip of my gun. Cal joins us with a delighted smile and presses the button for the top floor. Gears grind arthritically, but the elevator moves. Sounds like a goddamn stampede of elephants while it does, too.

"Finally, some peace and quiet," Cal says. "To get to your beloved point, I put Russ under with the Russians. Updates are sporadic, and for a tick there, it seemed dead likely he'd left this Earth. Day I called you, he let me know he'd just been given access to a base of operations inside the city itself. Address and all. Looks like our cold-blooded brethren are planning an invasion."

My stomach drops to the ground floor. Most bastards I can handle. The Russians scared my dad. If I went my whole life without fucking with them, I'd be happy.

The elevator rattles to a stop, and Cal shoulders the door open. Cool wind whips across the rooftop as we step out.

"And that very base is"—Cal scans the horizon, then points—"there."

A telescope and a set of binoculars sit facing that direction. I stride over and pick up the binoculars.

"So you're inviting us on a fishing trip."

Cal grins. "Settle in, gents."

THE SKY IS TURNING gray with morning by the time I seriously think about killing Cal Duncan. My knees ache, my eyes burn, and the scar where Domino opened me up is none too pleased. And we haven't seen jack shit.

I stretch and lean away from my binoculars. "I think—"

"Dante." Tony lifts the camera he brought along as a car pulls up.

I crush my eyes back to the lenses. The white convertible stops in front of the warehouse. It looks vaguely familiar. I crane forward, but there are no plates. This person knows where they are. The passenger door opens, and a broad-shouldered, heavily tattooed man gets out. I don't recognize him, so I train my binoculars on the driver's side. The person in there leans over to kiss the man goodbye, obscuring her face. My fingers start to hurt. A head of blonde hair comes into view, as well as a phone. The pieces start to click.

As the car speeds away, the driver hits a button to push back the convertible top, and I see Camila, talking on the phone in the pre-dawn light.

3 9

———

LOUKOUMADES

Eleni

I BLINK awake in the morning with my mouth watering. Cold sheets. No Dante.

I check my phone and find the usual text. At Piacere today, had to leave early, news when he gets home. I drop my phone with a groan. My stomach grumbles. I think I spent all night dreaming about loukoumades, these honey puffs Mama used to make for my birthday, or whenever she was in a really good mood. The air even smells like them, as if I brought the memory from my dreams into reality.

If Dante was here, I could have convinced him to drive around to find some. Instead, I'm just going to have to throw myself on Seb's mercy. Or, more accurately, the mercy of Seb's alarm clock. He's rarely awake before noon.

My mood sours as I get dressed and discover my favorite T-shirt fell out of the laundry basket before it got taken this week, so it's still dirty. I pull on one of Dante's and scowl at myself in the mirror as I brush my teeth. Today sucks. Maybe I'll skip schoolwork and catch

189

up with a few of my capos instead. That gives me a chance to see Dante, at least.

I stomp down the stairs, and the smell of loukoumades seems to be getting stronger, like it's taunting me. I throw open a window in the foyer as if I can chase out imaginary smells.

"*Zouzouni?*"

Great, now I'm hallucinating Mama's voice too. I really must not have slept last night. I storm into the kitchen for coffee—

And pull up short. Mama stands at the stove in one of her favorite dressing gowns, tending a spitting saucepan full of oil. A plate of glistening loukoumades sits on the counter behind her. She stares at me, tears filling her eyes. I pinch myself. Nope, still there.

"Mama?" I say tentatively.

"*Zouzouni!*" She smiles so wide I think her lips might split.

I throw myself at her for a hug. She stumbles back a step, warning me to be careful, and hugs me with one arm while tending the oil with the other. Familiar sensations wash over me like a tidal wave, and suddenly, I'm crying. Sobbing in Mama's arms like I'm a little girl again, and someone made fun of my accent on the playground.

"You look so different," she murmurs, "and so much the same."

"I've missed you, Mama," I whisper.

She kisses me on the head. "As I have missed you, but if you don't let go soon, I'm going to ruin perfectly good loukoumades."

I laugh wetly and release her, then grab the paper-towel lined plate to her left and hold it out. We move together like clockwork, like we're finishing a last batch before the lunch rush. She pulls them out of the oil and stacks them in neat rows, I blot off the excess and drizzle the dough in honey syrup, then add them to the finished pile behind her. Tears streak down my face, and my chest aches, but this is just as good as her holding me. Maybe better, because this lets me imagine Baba yelling from the front to hurry up before he flips the sign to "open" and Christos burning his fingers when he tries to steal one.

When all the loukoumades sit, pretty as a magazine, on the counter, Mama throws both her arms around me.

"What are you doing here?" I ask.

"Is your mama no longer allowed to visit?" She laughs.

I shake my head. "I'm always happy to see you. But I didn't know —"

Realization strikes like a lightning bolt. The surprise Dante mentioned. The one I couldn't have until morning.

"Dante brought you here, didn't he?"

She pulls back to look at me. "He did. Called me up, and of course Theia Adriani answered the phone." She shakes her head. "There was so much scuffle about you having a young man she almost forgot to tell me what he said."

My face burns. "I don't know if I *have* him." What did Dante say on the phone? Is Theia Adriani just blowing things out of proportion?

Mama clicks her tongue and looks me over once more. "His plane ride. His house. His cooking oil." She plucks the front of my T-shirt. "His clothes. There is something about this man you're not telling me, *zouzouni*."

I bite my lip. On the phone, I only told her Dante had taken me out a few times. It's way harder to hide how intertwined our lives are with her standing in our kitchen. His kitchen. Fuck.

"Is he stringing you along?" Thunderous fury crosses her face with such intensity that I'm briefly scared for Dante, surrounded by guards in his club.

I shake my head furiously. "No, Mama. I know he cares for me. And I know there's no one else." No matter what I yelled at him about yesterday."

She narrows her eyes. "Tell me how much a flight from Greece costs."

"Um, a couple hundred dollars each way?" I guess.

"Perhaps." Her intense stare doesn't relax. "And a private plane? Because I have not flown commercially since this man entered your life."

"Oh, that's no big deal," I say. "Dante already owned the plane."

She purses her lips in a way that tells me that was not the right answer. Before she can ask about whatever kind of gas planes use, I grab a loukoumade and pop it in my mouth.

My eyes flutter shut as the honey bursts over my tongue. It's delicious, but it's so much more than that. Like Dante said the first day we met, the loukoumades are good because they taste like birthday mornings before school, waking up in the winter dark and not resenting leaving the warmth of my blankets for once.

We made them for The Greek Corner always, but we ate them on birthdays and good days, so they taste like Baba loudly messing up the tune to the English birthday song because it's different in Greek and Mama humming to soft rock on the radio. They taste like a home I've barely had time to miss in months.

I open my eyes, and Mama is smiling at me like she can read my mind. I want those moments back.

"I'm his girlfriend," I blurt. "Dante loves me. And… and I love him."

4 0

WHY?

Eleni

MAMA DOESN'T LIKE the news I've fallen in love with Dante, judging by the lecture that follows. Still, I sit politely and listen to every word, smiling at the sheer joy of having a mother to scold me again.

After that, we talk over police procedurals, her favorite show and how to watch them, for a few hours, catching up on everything we haven't had time for in our last few calls.

Gianna shows up because I forgot we made lunch plans, and unlike Dante, Mama took to her instantly. Before an hour passes, she has Gianna in the kitchen with her hair pulled back, walking her through the steps of properly seasoning lamb for gyros. I sit at the kitchen island, correcting Gianna's technique when Mama isn't fast enough. She smacks my hand away when I try to steal a bite of pita, and for a moment, I think I know what it was like to be Christos when we were kids. She means the smack, but so much affection sparkles in her gaze that I know I have nothing to worry about. My heart squeezes. I should tell her about him.

Gianna tries to add basil to the lamb, and the moment passes. Mama and I smack her hand in unison.

Eventually, Gianna leaves for work—an explanation of which makes Mama press her hand primly over her mouth—and Mama and I drop back down onto the couch. Jet lag makes her fade fast, so I convince her to order an early dinner instead of cooking, and before the sun even sets, I have to rouse her from sleep in front of the TV.

"Mama," I say.

"Hm?"

I shake her shoulder gently. "You're going to hurt your neck."

"You worry too much, *zouzoui*." She swats my hand away. "You should see what Adriani had me sleep on. Pah."

"Then you deserve a nice bed." I kiss her cheek. "Please?"

Her eyes flutter open sullenly. "The same one as last time? It was nice and firm."

I bite my lip. "That one…actually got moved to a different room."

She sits up, sensing something she won't like. "Why?"

"For my office," I say truthfully.

"And where do you sleep now?" She eyes me critically.

"In another bedroom at the end of the hall?" I smile and hope she lets it go.

"Ah! I received the warnings about which doors not to open as well." She covers her mouth. "*Zouzouni*, you are sleeping in his bed?"

"He moved out for a little," I grumble.

That sets Mama off on a whole new string of questions, and I barely get her upstairs before she starts lecturing me on safe sex. Denying that we're sleeping together any way other than literally doesn't seem to get me anywhere, so I start promising we're being safe instead. This brings on a third tizzy. She is still lecturing me through the door as she changes into her pajamas.

"Yes," I mumble. "I understand."

She opens the door abruptly and meets my gaze. Tears fill her eyes. "I love you. Please take care of yourself."

I smile and hug her. "I am, Mama. You'll see."

"Tell him he ought to marry you," she says severely, even as her eyelids droop.

"I will."

That, finally, calms her, and she shuts the door to go to sleep. I putter around the house, picking at schoolwork, cleaning up the remains of dinner. The time Dante usually gets home passes. I text him. Nothing. I text a few capos. A few variations of "busy day, let the boss tell you." I roll my eyes and dick around on my laptop instead. For my own amusement, I code a crappy Staten Island Saints website that will never see the light of day.

The front door opens, and I hop up.

"El?" Dante calls tiredly.

I race to the foyer. His tie already hangs loose, his hair is mussed, and dark bags underline his eyes. No injuries, at least.

"Long day?" I bounce on my toes, trying to figure out how to balance his exhaustion with my excitement.

"Long day." He pulls off his tie and starts trudging upstairs.

I bound after him. "I got my surprise."

He smiles at me tiredly. "Yeah? How did you like it?"

"Like it?" I skip ahead of him to the landing, unable to stay still. "I love it. I love her. I love you!"

"Careful," he says. "Your surprise might hear you."

"She's already passed out from jet lag." I smile as he reaches me. "And I already told her."

He chuckles. "How did she take the news?"

"Better than I hoped." I grab his hand and struggle not to drag him down the hall. "Only two lectures!"

"That's nearly a recommendation," Dante says.

We traipse into the room in companionable silence.

"Why did you do this?" I ask.

He sits down on the bed, cups my face, and drags a thumb over my cheek. "Because I know you missed her. She can stay for longer than a visit, if you like. I've been thinking of installing a pool house out back for a while now, and her living here would be a great kick in the ass."

I turn my face and press a kiss to his palm. My heart is so full it feels like it might explode. "That's very sweet, but it's not what I'm asking."

He frowns as he pulls off his jacket and tosses it on the bed. "No? Then what?"

"I mean…." I look around. "Why all of this? Me living here? Tandon? Mama? She thinks I ought to tell you to marry me, with all you're doing for us."

Dante looks up at me with something warm brimming in his dark eyes. "Maybe she's right. Maybe I'm doing all this because I intend to marry you one of these days."

Mostly, when Dante and I fall into bed together, it's because one of us says something incendiary. I'm used to him lighting me ablaze with want or anger or petty drive to beat him. This confession only makes me warm. But it's a steady warmth, one that reminds me of the fireplace of a well-loved house or a campfire in the dark. Something I could follow home.

I straddle Dante's lap and kiss him.

41

YES

Eleni

DESPITE HOW TIRED he seemed a moment ago, Dante comes alive when I kiss him. He grips my hips like the last anchor in a storm, and I undulate against him like the waves he's trying to hold on through. I don't know what to do with this warmth in my chest. It's something more permanent than love, more certain. So I just wrap myself around him, slide my hands into his hair, and try to find a place where everything makes sense to me again.

Dante pulls back. "I'm a little sore tonight. I don't know if I have the whole routine in me."

That home-warmth flares.

"Okay," I say. "I don't mind."

He smiles against my lips. "I love you."

"I love you too." A giggle bursts from my lips. "Do you want me to…?"

Dante trails his kisses away from my mouth, down my neck. "Only if you need it. I'm happy just to feel you tonight."

He's nearly liquid underneath me, languorous and slow. I shake my head. I've never seen this side of Dante, not straining against his own iron control or forgetting about it completely but slumping out of it, discarding it like a set of clothes he doesn't need anymore. It feels dangerous, like the warmth in my chest does, and I have to know more.

I begin unfastening the buttons on his shirt slowly, running my hands over every new inch of bare skin. I savor the coil of his chest hair, the taut muscle underneath. He groans against my neck. When the cloth falls open, I push it off his shoulders. He releases me only long enough to pull it off his wrists, then holds onto my hips again.

With a smile, I lean my weight against him, pressing him down onto the bed. He goes without complaint and slides his hands under my T-shirt. I expect him to go for my bra, to crank the inferno that usually burns between us by teasing my nipples, but he just caresses my rib cage as if mapping the territory there. I grind against him, and he returns one hand to my hips to slow me.

"Can't keep up, grandpa?" I ask teasingly.

Dante looks up at me with eyes so full of the same warmth expanding my chest that all my jokes die a quick, painless death. He doesn't have to say anything for me to know he'll indulge anything I want to say, but he's not playing tonight. This is serious.

Whatever serious means to a man like Dante Cattaneo. My heart hammers, and I try to relax into his touch.

He carefully avoids my now well-known ticklish spots, and after long moments of raising every inch of my skin to total awareness, he tugs on the bottom of my skirt. I pull it off, feeling unbalanced.

Dante eases his hands up over my breasts now, contained in a thankfully modest bra for the day I've had. He still looks at it like the holy grail. This time, I expect another round of slow, teasing touch, but he unsnaps my bra quickly and tosses it aside. Then, he traces a finger delicately over the newly exposed skin, and I realize he has no time for clothes. He just wants to see me. My face burns. I don't know if I've ever been looked at so intensely, even by him.

"Don't get shy," he murmurs. "You're stunning."

I rock my hips against his. "It would be a lot easier not to if I wasn't alone."

"Soon." He smiles. Then, he traces the same path with his mouth that his hands followed moments ago.

I pant, feeling like a live wire. Everywhere he touches feels completely new. As if his focus has bled into me, I can't help noticing little details about Dante I never have before. I knew his nose had been broken, but there's a matching bump in his cheekbone, like someone busted his whole face. His knuckles are dusty with faded, overlapping scars, like he's scraped them so many times the injuries blended together. His dark eyes hide the barest hints of something lighter, flickers of brown or gold that catch the light every so often.

When Dante adjusts, pulling both of us farther onto the bed, I startle. I'd fallen so deep into studying him that I almost forgot he wasn't some old master's self-portrait but a real, live man who loves me.

"Still there?" he asks.

I nod. He offers me a quiet smile, and his teasing hands circle to the button of my pants. I lift off him for a moment to slide my shorts and underwear off in one motion. Then, I do the same to him. We're moving so slowly that I almost expect him not to be ready yet, but like the wetness dripping down my bare thighs, he's proudly hard. Still, I straddle him and just rock for a moment, not wanting to leave long enough to get a condom. Dante runs his hands up and down my bent legs, a promise he's just as happy as I am.

"Now," he says finally. "I can't wait any longer."

I lean over to grab a condom. Something behind me rustles, likely Dante adjusting again. When I turn back, he is higher on the pillows, though I have the vague sense something else moved as well. The thought floats out of my brain as I open the package and slide the protection onto his cock. He thrusts into my hand slowly, and I smile.

Dante lines me up, holding my gaze. "All at once?"

"Please," I whisper.

He pulls me down onto him, and with a pleasant burn, my hips meet his. I roll against him without lifting, and my eyes flutter closed.

More rustling.

"El?" Dante says.

I open my eyes. His jacket lays half on his chest, and in his hands, the ring box I spotted weeks ago sits open. Two slim, silver and gold bands sit inside. One hides blue stones in the crevices between where the two metals weave together, and the other, bigger one is plain. My breath catches.

"Marry me?" he asks.

That dangerous feeling yawns. Like standing at the edge of a cliff and wanting to jump. There's no turning back from this.

But I passed turning back a while ago. The warmth in my chest spreads to the tips of my fingers and toes.

"Yes." I kiss him.

As soon as I pull back, Dante whoops like a college boy and rolls me over. A wild smile paints his face. He fucks me into the mattress with celebratory thrusts, and I match his rhythm, laughing. Dante Cattaneo. My fiancé.

After all that build-up, my orgasm hits suddenly and sends me reeling. A moment after, Dante collapses onto my chest, panting.

"Two rings?" I ask as soon as I can. "Wedding and engagement?"

He smiles. "One for you, one for me. I promised."

I kiss him again.

4 2

BEST-LAID PLANS

Dante

THE NEXT MORNING, Eleni lies splayed across my chest, her naked shoulders peeking above the blanket. Her hand lays open, and the ring I picked out for her glitters on her finger. I smile. It was time. Being "just a girlfriend" in this life put her in so much more danger. At least, that's what I told Tony and the other guys. But who the fuck was I kidding? The birds are singing, the sun is shining, and my fiancée is drooling a little. My ribs hurt with how full my heart is.

Or with the weight said fiancée is putting on my still only mostly healed bullet wound. But I'll let El wake up in her own time. I brush a few curls back off her face.

She wakes up with a snort and blinks up at me in total confusion for a second. Then, she touches the corner of her mouth where the drool was coming from and turns bright red.

"It's okay!" I try to say before she can freak out.

She buries her head beneath the pillow. "Forget the proposal. I'm moving to Alaska."

I roll over top of her, caging her with my arms. "It's okay, really. I think it's kind of cute."

She peeks one eye out. "Think? Not thought? As in, this has happened more than once?"

I open and close my mouth helplessly. She groans and hides deeper underneath the pillow. But today, of all days, I'm not letting her run away from me. I pull the pillow off and expose her to my eyes, sleep-rumpled hair, drool, and all.

She's still red, but she's giggling a little now. I kiss her and barely notice neither of us have brushed our teeth yet. Forever like this. I could get used to that. She winds her arms around my neck, and the blankets shift, allowing me to feel her bare skin. Fuck, waking up to her naked is even better. I run my hands up her rib cage.

Eleni pulls back. "I have a small confession."

My heart skips a beat. "Yeah?"

"I saw the ring box a couple weeks ago." She bites her lip. "Were you planning a proposal for weeks and the best you could come up with was 'while you were inside me?'"

My mouth falls open. "You have notes already?"

"No, no!" She kisses me before I can move away in mostly mock hurt. "I was just curious."

I shake my head and roll off of her. By the amusement in her face, she really is just teasing. A few weeks ago. When did I fuck up? How is she so much smarter than me?

"I had a much bigger plan," I admit. "There was dinner, dancing, a trip to the back room where I bought you in Piacere."

She laughs. "How romantic."

I nudge her playfully. It would have been. "That's why I brought your mom here." I sit bolt upright. "Fuck. I was supposed to ask her permission."

"Old-fashioned." She plays with the hair on my chest. "Baba would've liked that."

She gets a faraway look in her eyes, and I kiss her once more.

"My parents would've loved you."

"Really?" She smiles. "I imagined your mom would've been the 'no one's good enough for my son' type."

"Oh, she was." I get out of bed and pull El with me. Our rings clink together. It feels a little silly, already wearing mine, but I promised, and I never want to break a promise to her. "I just think you'd have won her over anyway."

She starts getting dressed. "Is it my total mental breakdown after you got shot, or my lack of homemaking skills that would impress her?"

I smack El's ass as she pulls on a long, loose skirt. "Your blistering intellect, and the fact that you take no shit from me."

She laughs. "Mama will like you better if you curse less."

I mime locking my lips with a key and put on my suit as quickly as possible. Despite everything, work awaits. The very idea pains me. When we're both dressed, I grab El.

"Seriously," I say. "The impulsive proposal was good? Because we can still do the whole thing and not tell anyone you already said yes."

She meets my gaze, and her beautiful blue eyes overflow with emotion. It's not just protection for either of us.

"It was perfect." She kisses me. "I love you."

"I love you too." I grin and take her hand. "Now let's go see if I can impress your mom."

Maria is already awake and leaning over something sizzling on the stove when we come down.

"I'm making omeletta, *zouzou*—" She turns and sees the two of us, hand in hand. "Ah. Good morning, Dante."

"Good morning, Mrs. Calimeris." I resist the odd impulse to bow. Fuck, if I didn't already know I was in deep. I want this woman to like me so badly.

"Mama." El takes her hand from mine. "You know what you told me to tell Dante?"

She turns back to the stove. "That he ought to marry you if he wants to keep staking his claim like this."

Eleni holds out her hand. A beat of silence passes. Then another. Maria turns and sees the ring. She looks from it, to me, to El, to it again. She drops her spatula on the floor and swoops Eleni up in a hug.

They exchange a rapid, high-pitched mix of Greek and English that I can't parse, but it seems excited. While they celebrate, I wander around the kitchen island and pull out another spatula for when Maria inevitably notices the oven is still on.

Abruptly, she turns to me and looks me up and down. "Eleni tells me you have no family."

I swallow and set the spatula on the counter. "I have a cousin, and some friends I've grown up with."

She stares at me a moment longer. "What do you want out of a marriage?"

I glance at Eleni over her shoulder, who nods. No cursing.

"My mom and dad loved each other very much, but they were always on different pages," I say. "They lived their own lives in the same house. I don't want that." I look between the two women and realize for the first time that they have the exact same blue eyes. "I want a partner in life. Someone I share everything with. Who I lean on, and who leans on me."

Another beat of silence. Then, Maria sweeps me up in a bone-crushing hug.

"You'll call me Mama," she says. "I won't accept anything else after the wedding, but you should practice now."

I was wrong. My chest could ache with more emotion. I hug her back and don't consider the last time I hugged my own mother.

"Mama, the omeletta!" Eleni says.

Maria—Mama releases me instantly and turns to the stove.

<hr>

AFTER BREAKFAST, Gianna arrives. The ring is greeted with much squealing, and she whisks Eleni and Mama away for a spa day before I can get a word in edgewise. For a moment, I think I've lost my cousin to the allure of actually having women in my house, but she pauses at the door and punches me in the shoulder.

"Took you long enough," she says.

I laugh. "Did you really think I would let this one go?"

"If she asked you to." Gianna shakes her head. "Congrats. Don't fuck it up."

With that good luck, I head back inside and dial Tony.

"Dante," he answers quickly.

My news hums on my tongue, but I have something more important to ask first. "Did you figure out what Camila was doing?"

His sigh is harsh over the line. "She didn't make it back to the apartment. I put a couple other guys on her tail, but she knows these fucking streets. Dumped her convertible and lost them on foot."

"Motherfucker." I spin my ring around my finger as the heavy mantle of boss settles back on my shoulder. The news can wait. I have to figure out what the fuck Camila is doing talking to the Russians.

4 3

HERE AND GONE

Eleni

A WEEK AFTER MAMA ARRIVED, we walk along South Beach with our sandals in our hands, looking out over the water at the Verrazano.

"—and then Adriani said, 'if you get another orange from that man, I'm going to nail them to his front door and let the streets run orange with the juices!'" Mama says.

I laugh so hard I actually have to stop walking. The sand burns my feet, but I don't mind. Mama and I have spent nearly every day together since she arrived, and as much as she complains about Theia Adriani, she tells stories about her younger sister almost constantly.

"Theia Adriani should meet Tony," I say when I get my breath back. "I think they'd either fall passionately in love or hate each other on sight."

Mama smiles. "Tony is the one with the very stiff hair, yes? And those lovely eyes."

I swallow down another burst of laughter and decide to tell everyone about the "stiff hair" comment later. "Yes, he is."

She nods. "And he is the right hand. Capo supreme."

207

"*Caporegime,*" I correct.

"Of course." She looks out at the bridge. "You are happy here, *zouzouni?*"

I take a deep breath. The ring still sits heavily on my finger, the blue stones catching the light off the sea and glittering. Being engaged feels strange, half-real and half a dream. I'm not unhappy. God, I can't imagine being unhappy right now. Mama and I have spent a week—with Gianna almost more often than not—doing all the expensive things in the city we always talked about when I was younger and never dreamed of actually doing.

Every night, I've come home to Dante, knowing my place was beside him in bed, and usually come a few times before even considering sleep. It's like a vacation from reality. I haven't felt this light on my feet since I got into community college and Mama and Baba said they could pay for my first semester if I went part-time. I tug on the tracking necklace I've been wearing again since I got engaged and nod.

"Good," she says decisively. "Because I have been thinking it is time for me to go home."

I blink. "What?"

She takes my free hand and looks at me. "I love seeing you, *zouzouni,* but I have seen Parikia through an old woman's eyes now. My little seaside home is not so cramped as I feared when I was young. It is beautiful, and so much of my family is there."

I feel like someone's punched a hole in my chest. "I...I told you about the pool house, right?"

"You did." She smiles indulgently. "Your Dante is very kind to the both of us. But I don't think I belong in your back pocket anymore. You'll simply have to come visit."

"I know where Christos is buried," I blurt.

Mama takes a step back. "What?"

My stomach churns. I wasn't supposed to say it like this. I don't know if I was supposed to say it at all.

"Upstate." I blink back sudden tears. "He was...there was a raid. He got caught in the crossfire. Dante...found him. They were friends in college, so Dante took care of his body. And I know where."

She puts a hand to her heart. Her own tears spill, hot and painful. "I will see him."

I nod. "Just stay a little longer, and I'll take you."

"Don't do this to me, *zouzouni*," she pleads. "I can't live two lives. Let me return to the place where my family has not been killed after one last goodbye."

I stare at her for a long moment. My heart feels like it's being torn in two. I missed Mama even worse than I thought, and the idea of being alone here again aches.

My ring catches the light. I suppose I'm not really alone anymore. Dante will become my family. And with him, Gianna. Tony and Seb, in their own ways. The other capos I've earned the loyalty of. Maybe my world isn't so small that I need a Calimeris in New York City not to be lonely anymore.

I wrap my arms around Mama. "Okay. But you're coming back for the wedding."

She squeezes me. "I would not dream of anything else."

After a long moment, I release her, and we don't need to say anything to realize it's time to return to the car and drive home. The sun has started sinking over the horizon, and dinner with Dante has become tradition.

Mama keeps interrogating him about what she calls "his character" and what I call "whatever she might disapprove of," a game Dante has survived very bravely so far. Maybe she'll ask about Christos tonight. I don't know what he'll say. Part of me wishes I'd told the truth about his death, but the rest keeps a picture of his face, drawn in pain, begging Dante not to tell his family. I needed the truth, but Mama only needs to know Christos isn't lost. I won't take her memories from her.

We reach my car, and I scan my surroundings like I've grown used to doing over these months with the Saints. An older couple, sharing a single ice cream cone in the summer heat. A few children screaming on a playground. Two teenagers, making out in a place they clearly think no one can see them. Only a few cars. One of the cars catches my attention. It's a late-model sedan, dull brown-gray, like a million others. But I feel like I've seen it before.

Before I can puzzle out where, the door opens, and a dark-haired man in a suit gets out and looks at me.

"Get in the car, Mama," I say without looking at her.

"What? *Zouzouni*—"

I hand her the keys. "Get in the car."

She obeys without another work. The car roars to life, and I circle around it to meet the man a few feet away.

"You've been following me," I guess before he says anything.

"I'm new to town," he replies. "Or old to town, but I've been away for a while. You're Eleni, aren't you?"

I look him up and down. Black suit, white shirt, dark blue tie. Completely nondescript, like something a politician would wear. But I know enough now to notice how the suit doesn't quite fit him, like he's just about an off-the-rack size and doesn't have the time or money for a tailor. He wears heavy, rubber-soled shoes that look like office shoes, for if he needs to run. His underarm bulges with the tell-tale shape of a shoulder holster.

"I might be," I say. "That depends on who's asking."

"Henry Alcott." He flicks a card out of his jacket pocket and hands it to me. "A wayward branch of the Bellini line, if you can believe it. They say I have the nose."

I take the card but keep my gaze on Henry. Bellini means Tony and Seb, but I don't see any of their good looks in this man. Well, maybe in the nose. It could be Roman, in the right light.

"I just wanted to offer my congratulations," he says.

My heart skips a beat as he glances at my ring. "Thank you. We're very happy."

"I'm always glad to welcome someone new to the family." Henry leans in as if to kiss me on the cheek but leaves an inch of air between his lips and my skin. "I'm just here to make introductions, so I'll let you and your mom get back to your day."

Without another word, he turns and walks away, his oversized jacket flapping in the breeze off the water. I slide into the driver's seat of my car, confused and off-kilter.

"Who was that man?" Mama asks. "Are you in danger?"

"Henry Alcott." I look down at the crisp card in my hand, and the square, black print turns my stomach. "Special Agent, Organized Crime."

4 4

SAYING GOODBYE

Dante

I STAND on the porch of my safe house upstate, fidgeting with my watch.

When Eleni told me she mentioned Christos to Mama, I nearly stopped breathing. I expected demands for answers about why I killed her son. I didn't expect tearful requests for his last words, college stories, and to leave from the airstrip upstate when she returned to Greece a few days later.

I can just see the two of them through the trees, standing in front of the half-hidden grave. Eleni holds Mama, and both of them shake. For the first time in a week, I can actually forget about Camila. I stand on the edge of a towering, personal grief, knowing I was the one who caused it. Still, I'm never really sure if I regret shooting Christos. I miss the devil-may-care freshman, the once-in-a-generation running back, the bastard who made me laugh and carved a line through parties with me. I fucking hate the memory of the taste of his blood, the gunpowder that stained my hands for what felt like weeks after.

But the Christos I shot wasn't really the one they loved anymore. And now at least Mama gets to keep her vision of them intact.

Finally, the two of them rejoin me on the porch with puffy eyes and straight backs. Whatever happened out there is not for me to know.

"Ready?" I ask.

El nods. "As I'll ever be."

Mama squeezes her hand, and we head out to the car together. Luckily, the drive to the airstrip isn't long. My pilot bitched about the fifteen-minute flight upstate, but I just told him to call it an extra hour spent flying to Greece, and that quieted him down. We pull up to the small tarmac, and Maria looks at Eleni.

"I love you," she says. "You must come visit."

Eleni smiles tightly. "I love you too, Mama. And we will. Just as soon as I know how my first semester is going to go."

Mama smiles. "My daughter, NYU. I always knew you were the smart one."

I flex my fingers on the wheel and try not to intrude. Despite her interrogation, Mama seems to be warming to me, but I know this is their moment.

Suddenly, she says. "You will get my bags, yes, Dante?"

I switch off the car. "Of course."

Eleni hugs her one last time, and she and I get out. I unload her two bags from the trunk and start heading for the plane.

"You were friends," she says quietly, in the voice I've come to recognize means she's talking about Christos or her husband. "Was he...?"

She doesn't have to end the question. I know she's asking if he joined my line of work.

"No," I say. The best lie I've ever told sparkles through the morning air as her shoulders slump in relief.

"Don't tell Eleni I thought that," she says. "Her brother was her hero. Just like my Gregorio. They only saw his sun shining."

I hand her bags to the flight attendant and turn to face her. "Eleni is tougher than you think."

She smiles tiredly. "Eleni is tougher than I am willing to admit to myself. But a mother's job is to protect her children, even after they stop needing it."

I chuckle. "That, I understand. What am I supposed to do as a husband with a wife like her?"

Mama looks at me steadily. "Just what I am doing. She can take care of herself, but she deserves the breaks. Give them to her, always."

"Every time." I open my arms for a hug.

She embraces me. "I am not kidding about the visit. I will make friends with your pilot and have him kidnap you, if I must."

"Deal." I kiss her on the cheek and let her go.

She boards the plane and waves once from the top of the stairs. I return to the car, and El.

"What did she say?" Eleni asks.

"To take care of you." I hold her hand as the plane taxis away.

"It doesn't feel like peacetime anymore, does it?" Eleni says after a long moment.

My temper flashes. She's talking about Henry Alcott, cornering her and Mama the other day. If I knew where he was staying, I would've punched his nose in for that alone, plans be damned.

She shakes her head as she sees my face. "Not just Henry. Whatever's going on with the Russians and Camila too."

I sigh. "No, it doesn't."

The plane takes off, and I pull out of the airstrip. We chat for the whole drive home, both of us avoiding the pronouncement that our quiet summer is ending. Eleni starts school in two weeks, and we have a wedding to plan. Things were going to be busy enough without whatever war is kicking up. So we try to hold onto these last few moments by planning the most extravagant, avant-garde wedding either of us can imagine.

"And then," Eleni says, "I'll swing in on the trapeze, and you'll catch me."

"No." I turn onto the street I've been looking for, deep in the city. "The priest, who is also on trapeze, will catch you and toss you through a ring of fire into the waiting arms of an ice sculpture of me."

She laughs. "Which will melt, because I've caught on fire, to reveal you inside. At which point—"

I pull into an underground garage and park in the spot labeled 1A. She glances around.

"Where are we?"

"You won't live on campus for the semester." I climb out of the car, walk to her side, and open the door. "But I don't want you commuting from Staten Island every day."

"Dante," she says warningly.

"Just let me show you." I smile.

She eyes me suspiciously but lets me lead her into the elevator, then use the key card to head to the second to top floor. The doors *ding* softly and open onto a stunning apartment I purchased fully furnished.

"We can change anything you like," I say as she drifts away from me. "But it's a five-minute walk to Tandon from here. You'd barely need to get up in time not to miss class."

"And you'll live on Staten Island?" She looks at the massive windows, the sunlight pouring in.

I shrug.

"I don't like it." She crosses her arms and turns back to me. "I'm not living away from you. You can't just cut me out of the Saints like this."

"Hey, I'm not cutting you out of anything." I rush across the living room and take her in my arms. "I'm going to have a lot more work in the city now that I've got all this Lombardi territory. I just didn't want to crowd you."

She purses her lips. "But you'll still be there sometimes."

"Piacere is on the island." I sigh. "It's not a perfect solution. But did you really want to take the ferry every day?"

She looks around. "I'll come home on weekends. And—"

My phone rings. Tony. El falls silent as I pick up the call.

"Get here," Tony barks. "Yesterday."

45

SHOTS FIRED

Eleni

I STAND on the wrecked stage of Piacere and turn in a slow circle. The two bars glisten under thick drifts of broken glass, and puddles of spilled alcohol drool away from them. Not a table stands upright. More than half of them are splintered. Under the brilliant daytime lights of the club, goosebumps pepper my skin. It feels like looking at a ghost.

It feels like looking at The Greek Corner, the day after Baba's murder and my rescue, when Tony took me back.

Dante storms up the stairs. "They took a good fucking chunk out of the basement, but either they couldn't find the secret door, or they couldn't get through."

His eyes dance with rage. I step over one of the poles, ripped from its mooring to lean against the stage, and close the distance between us. Still, I don't touch him. There's an electricity radiating off him that I can't catch up with yet. My anger feels dull, faraway. It's too much like that day, the day my whole life changed, for me to touch it yet.

"Anyone hurt?" I ask.

"Massimo," he says. "The bartender. Clubbed with a bottle of whiskey when he went for the gun under the bar."

I suck in a breath through my teeth. Massimo is a new hire, made under my reign. I promised him this was just a club. This is my fault.

"It doesn't make any fucking sense," Dante continues. "Four dancers in the back. Carla in the upstairs office. They swept through the whole goddamn place, if the matchsticks I have for furniture are anything to go by, but they only hit Massimo."

"Is he okay?" I ask.

Dante waves my words away. "Domino's en route. He's conscious."

Not dead. I exhale sharply. "You said there were other people? Did they see anything?"

He whirls on me. "Do I look like I'm in the mood to play fucking good cop, bad cop right now? You go fucking talk to them, if you care so goddamn much."

Like a spark on paper, my numbness burns away. I shove Dante. He doesn't move.

"Watch who you're fucking talking to like that," I spit. "I'm going to go talk to your goddamn people who were attacked in your goddamn club and see if I can get something more useful than a fucking attitude out of them."

I don't give him time to respond, just turn on my heel and march into the back. Carla will be with the dancers at this point, making sure they're okay. And Dante will cool the fuck down if I give him a second. Let him take his rage out on a broom if he's so pissed.

The door to the dressing room stands open when I reach it, and I duck in to find Gianna with Crystal, Sabrina, and Tiff in the corner, and Carla furiously typing on her laptop next to them. When she sees me, Gianna bursts from the huddle of dancers and throws herself at me. I wrap her in a hug.

"What the hell happened?" I ask.

"We were just getting ready," she says. "We didn't even know anything was happening until the big crash."

"Crash?"

Carla meets my gaze. "The first bar, I suspect. I heard the doors burst open. Which means I had the chance to intervene before they hit Massimo, and these young women did not."

Gianna releases me and whips around. "Don't do that. If you tried to get involved, they'd have hit you too."

"Or worse," Sabrina adds.

Carla returns to glaring at her laptop. "Does this mean Dante is here?"

I nod.

"Good," she says. "I have information for him."

She starts to stand, and I put up a hand.

"He's in a bitchy mood. Give me the information, and I'll let him know when he's less likely to blow up."

She purses her lips. "Will he not blow up at you?"

"I know how to handle him." I smile wanly.

As one, the dancers look at my hand. Despite the fear still quivering through most of their limbs, my engagement pulls attention. I know Gianna told them. I just haven't had time to go to Piacere since it happened.

I sit on the floor with them and hold out my hand for them to admire as we talk. "Did any of you see anything?"

"Three men," Carla says.

"Four," Gianna corrects. "But two of them were twins or so damn similar it doesn't matter, and they tried to stay apart."

Carla inclines her head. "They dragged us all out into the middle of the club."

"It was only half-destroyed." Crystal's lower lip quivers. "When they made us sit. We had to watch while they did the rest. And they had us sit back to back and shot the ceiling if we moved."

"They had guns, but they didn't use them?" I ask.

"Not on us," Carla replies.

I frown. She nods in agreement.

"It was kind of like they wanted to be scary, but not messy," Gianna says. "Like they didn't want any more clean up than would cost a fuckload of money."

"Okay." I nod slowly. "And what did they look like?"

Everyone starts talking at once. I pick out a few details. All white men. Mostly tall and broad. One with bad teeth. All of them were bald. No, one had a ponytail. The twins moved like the same person. Carla puts up her hand, and the rest of them fall silent.

"They had tattoos," she says. "And I'm writing down everything I can remember about them now."

I take a deep breath in relief. Tattoos, we can use. The rest could be feds—doubtful, but it could be—or the Irish, or the Russians, or some enemy we don't even know about yet. I put out my hands, and Carla gives me her laptop. I skim the lines of text quickly and feel the blood drain from my face.

"Russians," I say.

Gianna winces. The rest of the dancers murmur amongst themselves.

"Okay." I give Carla back her laptop and stand. "I'm going to go talk to Dante. I'd bet we're going to be closed tonight, so if Gianna took all of you to that spa in the city we went to with Mama the other day, I could find a way to get that paid for."

Gianna pats my leg. "You're a good boss."

I laugh, half out of overwhelm, and head back out to the front of the club. Dante stands in the middle of the mess with Tony, pointing people in this direction and that as clean-up begins. I walk right up to him.

"It's the Russians," I say.

"I fucking know that," he snaps.

I raise an eyebrow at him. He takes a deep breath.

"How are they?" he says quietly.

"They're going to a spa," I reply. "You're paying."

Tony snorts. Dante punches him, then kisses me on the cheek.

"Thank you, El. You're right."

I grin, partially at Tony, and take in the mess of the club again. Now, having made sure everyone I love is safe this time, it looks less like The Greek Corner. It looks more like a fucking insult I can't wait to pay back. The old anger simmers back to life in my veins.

"So who's the boss of the Russians?" I ask.

"Count Dracula," Tony replies.

"Stupid name." I smile. "He'll—"

Dante shakes his head. "Tony's being a dick. We don't...know, exactly."

I stare around me, my stomach sinking. Whoever this was stepped onto our territory, messed up our shit, and we have no idea who to hit back?

"Don't worry, El." Dante wraps an iron arm around my waist. "We're going to find out. And they're going to fucking pay."

46

TURNABOUT

Dante

I CHECK the cylinder on my second pistol—full—and slide it back into place with a *click*. Adrenaline courses through my veins as I put my eye to the sniper sight Tony set up on the apartment roof across from the Russian warehouse Cal showed us.

"We're trusting Cal Duncan?" Tony asks.

"You got another fucking option?" I reply.

His sharp sigh behind me tells me I've already won. I knew I was going to. If we give the Russians more than twenty-four hours, we look weak. But we don't know shit about their operations, other than this warehouse. Assuming Cal was telling the truth. And if I'm being honest, I think Cal's more likely to give us the warehouse of another syndicate, on the off chance he lied, so at least I don't have the deaths of civilians to worry about. I lean back from the sight.

Tony stands behind me, along with Seb and three other capos. Seb's just about vibrating out of his skin, being taken on an all-capo mission. Tony said it wasn't a good idea, but his induction is next weekend. He's already a made man, I just haven't announced it.

"Tony, Raf, take the side entrance," I say. "Mikey, Dice, the back. Seb and I have the front."

They nod, even Seb, who's struggling to stay professional. Mikey's not a capo I call in often. He lives with his wife in Paterson, just over the border into Jersey, and he's the capo I call when I think some shit I'm about to put my foot in might spill over to the families out there. I thought about just warning him, but I decided more guns would be better, and so many of my regular people are split between cleaning up Piacere and watching Eleni.

I check both my pistols one last time. Camila could be in there. I doubt it, but I can't be sure. Am I ready to kill her?

The ring on my finger shines dully in the darkness. El wasn't at Piacere, but she could've been and the last thing I need is Russians circling close to home. I'll do whatever I need to do.

"Move," I say.

We troop down through the building, out onto the street, then split into our three groups. Surveillance says there shouldn't be more than a couple dozen Russians. They might be crazy, but crazy doesn't have shit on planning. I pop an earpiece into my ear.

"Alpha."

"Beta," Tony answers.

"Sigma," Mikey mutters.

"Count of three," I say. "One."

Seb meets my eye, heft his semi-auto, and winks. It's like I'm taking him to an amusement park, not a firefight. It's kind of sweet.

"Two."

He takes aim at the doorknob.

"Three." I raise my gun, and we shoot the lock and knob in unison. The door swings jaggedly back.

Matching explosions on the other sides of the building tell me the other two teams did the same. I shoulder open the door, Seb on my heels, and storm inside. A bullet slices past my head and lodges in the cement wall behind me.

"Fuck!" Seb shouts.

Waste of energy. I dive behind one of the many shelves stacked with boxes and pull him with me. Gunfire echoes off the high ceiling, and I peer around a box to try to get a lay of the land.

The black muzzle of a rifle stares back at me. I whip behind the box just in time to feel two shots thud into it. Something white fills the air, and my heart skips a beat.

"Coke." I loosen my tie and yank my shirt up over my mouth and nose. "Watch your breathing."

Seb follows suit automatically. There are more Russians than I thought, and they're as balls to the wall as their reputation promises. I'd do almost anything before shooting the product. Still, the cloud gives some cover. I lean around the other side of the box and see a figure in something other than the all-black of my men moving. I squeeze off two shots. The figure jerks and falls with a Russian curse.

I smile. Seb starts to leave, and I whip around as he ducks back. With a smile, he shows me what he grabbed. A fucking pen.

"What—"

He launches it away from us, high, then scuttles to the side Tony's door isn't on. Smart. I follow him, escaping the cloud of drugs kicking my heart rate higher. We slide between shelves, and I take out another Russian. Seb, ahead of me, comes up behind a third and puts two bullets in the base of his spine before he can yell. I grin at him. I knew he could fucking handle this.

Away from the front door, we have a lot more space to play. Russians prowl forward, waiting for us to emerge from the cloud of cocaine. We slice through shelving units, circling them like avenging angels, and body after body falls at our feet. In the back of my mind, I note details. A couple of laptops on that table. Scales over there, next to plastic wrap and baggies. A drug operation, obviously. And a big enough one to warrant a warehouse rather than a basement. How the fuck didn't I notice this? The Saints only dabble in drugs—they're hard to justify, easy to get caught with, and less valuable than most of the luxury products we ship—but I try to keep an eye on the corners. Am I losing my fucking touch?

"Dante!" Seb shouts.

Yes, it seems, I am. I stopped in the middle of a fucking firefight to look at drug paraphernalia like a jackass. I turn toward the sound of Seb's voice in what feels like slow motion and spot the lanky, tattooed Russian the second after his gun goes off.

I finally have my life together. I'm happy. I'm looking forward to the future. Maybe this is why all the grizzled older bosses I've met have looked miserable. Maybe being miserable is the only way to survive this life. I close my eyes and wait for the pain.

Something slams into me, but not like a bullet. Like a fucking body that knocks me to the ground, jars my skull against the cement floor. The front of my suit grows wet, but nothing hurts. I pry open my eyes.

The something on top of me is Seb, bleeding heavily from the bullet spray across his chest. He fucking jumped in front of me. I meet Tony's gaze over the shoulder of the Russian who shot Seb, and I know the priorities have changed.

We have to get Seb out before he pays my price.

4 7

RACE AGAINST THE CLOCK

Dante

THE LANKY RUSSIAN advances on me, and I raise Seb's pistol because mine is pinned under his body. His fingers slip limply from the trigger, and I grimace as I land three shots in the Russian's chest. He drops like a sack of rocks. Tony skids through the haze of gun smoke to my side.

"Seb," he whispers urgently.

Seb's eyes roll aimlessly in his head. My heart hammers. Tony has no idea where his fucking gun is. It's my job, from underneath his bleeding brother, to keep all three of us alive. A much bigger Russian advances, wearing a set of brass knuckles, and I blow him away before his attention can lock on us.

"Sebastian Bellini." Tony takes his younger brother's head in his hands. "You have to fucking answer me, or I'm going to tell Nonna you've been missing her, and she should really call every day."

Seb coughs. "Dick."

Tony and I exhale matching gusts of relief. It's not over yet. Tony wedges his arms under Seb, keeping him as still as possible while I slide out. The front of my suit drips with his blood, but I swallow down the metallic stench I'm all too familiar with.

A Russian looms out from behind a shelf with—

"Is that a fucking grenade?" Tony hisses.

Fucking Russians. When Tony speaks, the Russian pulls the pin from the grenade with his teeth and cocks his arm back. I abandon Seb's gun and throw myself at the man holding the grenade. He's got a few inches on me and maybe fifteen pounds, but you don't play D1 football without learning how to fucking tackle, so we both hit the ground hard.

I slam my fist into his face. When he opens his mouth to yelp in pain, I snatch the pin from his teeth and shove it back in the grenade.

"Dante!" Tony yells.

I jump to my feet, stomp on the Russian's wrist to make him release the grenade, then grab the little bomb and stuff it in my pocket before racing back. Tony has Seb draped over his shoulder, but he's staggering under his brother's weight, and he can't protect himself in the middle of this chaos.

A figure appears in the smoke. I wheel, grabbing my second pistol, but it's just fucking Mikey.

"Seb's hit," I spit. "I have to help Tony. You clear us a path."

Mikey nods without a word. He towers over me, over even Seb, and his silent bulk is as much of a comfort as I think I can get in this bullshit. I slide my second pistol back and slip under Seb's other arm. Mikey strides ahead, and gunshots ring through the bleary fog. There's nothing Tony and I can do but trudge inexorably forward, dragging the weight of a kid we've both watched grow up, and pray Mikey's actually clearing the warehouse. Inch by painful inch, we move, leaving a trail of ruby-red blood behind us.

Like the proverbial light at the end of the tunnel, the front door Seb and I burst through scant minutes ago appears out of the haze. Mikey stands next to it, gun in hand. I pass him my second pistol as we make it outside. He needs the bullets more than me right now.

Seb, Tony, and I crumple to the street in a pile. Tony catches Seb, cushioning his fall, and cradles his head.

"What did you do for me?" I demand. "We can fucking fix this."

Tony rips open Seb's shirt and puts out a hand. I shuck my jacket and hand it to him like we've been doing this all our lives. Haven't we? But as I look at Seb's pale chest, my stomach sinks. According to Domino, I took one bitch of a shot in the lung. These Russians don't have that dignity. It looks like they hit him with fucking buckshot, but each of the dozen holes are as deep as a usual bullet.

Seb looks like goddamn mincemeat. I can barely see his skin because of the blood. But Tony still tries to apply pressure with my jacket, rotating between the different bullet holes like he doesn't know that means he's wasting his time.

"You listen to me, Sebastian," he hisses. "You're not going to fucking die like this. Do you even know you have plans next weekend? You were about to become a capo, you little shit."

Seb wheezes in a breath, and blood gouts out of him. I flinch.

"I'm going to tell everyone to call you Peaches." Tony's voice sounds ragged. "Or—or—"

"Love...you..." Seb manages. "T."

He slumps in his brother's arms. Tears sting the backs of my eyes, but as Tony bellows, a pure, animal sound of pain, my rage sings above everything else.

They can't do this to the Staten Island fucking Saints.

I yank Tony's spare gun from his waistband. He barely notices. I storm back, and Mikey silently hands me a semi-auto rifle instead of my pistol. I flick the safeties off each and wade into the horror show unfolding in the warehouse.

Bullets zing. I am a one man torch, a match that will bring the whole Russian organization down before the news of Seb's death reaches them. Before it reaches his fucking nonna. Bodies fall before me like I'm Moses parting the Red Sea. Sharp pain splits my shoulder. I don't care. I can still pull the goddamn trigger, and nothing matters more to me than that right now. Sebastian is dead. I told him how to kiss a girl when he was too embarrassed to ask Tony. I drove him to his prom. I brought him in the front fucking door.

The next thing I feel is Raf's hand on my uninjured shoulder. Slowly, his voice filters into my ears.

"...all done, boss. They're dead."

I drop the guns on the floor. Along with the voice, I can now hear the most irritating song I've ever heard in my life.

"Who is playing that?" I roar.

Raf points a little shakily to my pocket, where I can see the glowing screen of my phone. It's my goddamn ringtone. I rip the device out of my pants, and it takes all my willpower to answer the call instead of shattering the whole thing.

"Speak fast," I growl. "And have good news."

"Alas, I can only deliver on one front." Cal Duncan's brogue sounds a little strained. "Seems we were both hit. I've lost five men."

"For the last goddamn time," I say as calmly as I can muster, "I am not working with you, Duncan. I am never fucking going to be working with you. Call me again, and you'll lose more than five."

I hang up the phone and am about to drop it when it rings again. I slam the accept button.

"That's it, Dunca—"

"Dante?" Gianna asks breathlessly.

My heart crashes through the floor. Gianna doesn't call me unless there's a problem.

"Fuck it, I know it's you," she blurts. "The club's on fucking fire, Dino, and I don't know who's inside. I barely made it out."

My skin grows cold. Rage and panic war for supremacy. I manage one sentence.

"Where's Eleni?"

4 8

WARTIME

Eleni

I FLIP a page in my textbook, but the words blur in front of my eyes. Dante's out raiding his only lead on the Russians right now, trying to get any kind of thread that'll lead us to their boss. I helped clean up at Piacere as long as I could, but eventually, after the week with Mama and the emotional stress, I had to call it a night. I was hoping I'd get in a little studying so I could actually be ready when classes started in a few weeks, instead of waiting until things got crazier and crossing my fingers, but reading is proving harder than I hoped.

Ben, the son of Thano's capo who saved me during exams, leans into the doorframe. "How's it going?"

"Like shit." I lean back in my chair. "Thanks for taking me home anyway. At least this way I'm not doing a shit job with broken glass."

He chuckles. "It's my job, somehow. Heard you're leaving school, though. Going all in on the life?"

"Going to the Tandon Institute, actually." I close my textbook and hold it up so he can see the very official-looking cover.

He whistles. "Man, I'm half-glad Dante took out Thano Coppola when he did. I wouldn't want to go up against the Saints with a computer engineer on their team."

I smile tiredly. "I'm sorry about all that, by the way. The probation was—"

"Crappy," he supplies. "But I get it. You were put in an impossible position. I can't imagine going from no one to boss in a day."

I blow out a long breath. "It didn't feel that impossible at the time."

He snorts. "If you say so. I was going to make some popcorn. Want any?"

I nod. "I'll be down in a second anyway. I'm just wasting brain cells up here."

Ben flicks me a salute and ducks out of the door. I sit at my desk a moment longer and run my hand over the cover of the textbook. An impossible position. According to everyone, I shouldn't have been able to step into Dante's shoes as easily as I did. I've never asked, but I don't know whether they mean that I shouldn't have had the skills or the morals.

The Eleni that greeted the morning for those two weeks...she scares me. But I also know she lives tucked neatly under my skin, waiting for her next chance to shine. She's antsy tonight, in the wake of the attack on Piacere. Dante's the right person to lead a raid on a Russian warehouse. I—or she—is the right person to start hunting for leads on the Russians other ways. Maybe I'll take a brief break with Ben, then come back up here and see what I can find online. Even in those two weeks, I found a few ways onto parts of the Internet normal people rarely see. I stand.

Someone knocks. Probably Gianna. I promised her she could sleep here tonight, and I wouldn't put it past Dante to change the locks without mentioning it to me or her after a day like today. The door creaks open, and I hear Ben say something.

Pop.

For a split second, I think someone burst a balloon. Then, I remember Dante sitting me down and teaching me what gunshots sound like muffled. My heart slams into my throat. I reach under my desk—

And remember I took my gun to the bedroom to clean it in case they needed me tomorrow. It's been so quiet that I haven't been servicing the damn thing as often as I need to. I don't hear anything downstairs, but it's a heavy silence. Dense with possibility. I slide my slippers off and pray the door to the bedroom is already open so I don't have to worry about creaks. At least the leggings Gianna has finally convinced me into are nearly perfectly silent.

I creep around my desk and peer out the open door. No obvious sign of intruders, except the front door swinging open in the wind. Another *pop* echoes through the house, and I swallow down a wave of nausea. That sounded farther away. I think. So I slip out of my office and start down the hall. I pass one door, two, three. Then, I reach the open area of the hall, where I can be seen from the first floor, the foyer on one side and a sitting room on the other. I freeze, take a long breath. It's quiet. So goddamn quiet. I peek my head out.

Three massive men wearing dark masks with guns already drawn whip their heads up to stare at me from where they stand over the bleeding body of Andrea in the sitting room.

"Fuck." I sprint down the hall toward my gun.

Heavy footsteps pound after me. They shout back and forth to each other in a language I don't understand, Russian or some other Eastern European one. A few more gunshots go off, but the bullets don't hit anywhere around me. The door to the bedroom is within reach.

The floor under my feet jerks back, and I fall flat on my fucking face. It moves again, and I realize one of them made it to the top of the stairs and started pulling on the goddamn carpet. I snarl and scramble up. My gun is in my nightstand. Dante has one—fuck, I saw it earlier, where is it? Even a few inches closer might make the difference.

Pop. A bullet lodges in the drywall next to my head. My throat threatens a parched scream, but I don't indulge. Fuck Dante's gun. Mine is close enough.

One set of footsteps speeds up. *Thud, thud*—nothing. What?

Then, it hits me. Or should I say, he hits me. Three hundred pounds of Russian goon collides with my back in a flying leap, and I hit the ground so hard I feel something snap in my chest. Pain sparkles through my vision. He yells something triumphant.

The pain threatens to make me black out. The cold, sure Eleni of my two weeks without Dante slides out and snatches the reins from me.

I wriggle in his arms until I can face him, wrench one arm free with a smothered scream and claw at his face. My freshly painted nails catch on his eyelid, his cheek, and blood beads in my wake. He bellows and backhands me. More white stars of pain. Something knocks loose in my jaw. I spit a fountain of red into his face while fumbling around his belt with my other hand. A knife, a gun, anything to give me the edge.

Too little, too late. He snatches my hand and holds it out to the side. Another of them steps into my peripheral vision and shoots a hole clean through the center of my palm. Calm, confident Eleni slips away, and I howl.

The attacker on top of me climbs off just in time for me to watch, through tear-filled eyes, as the final man swings a baseball bat at my head.

STITCHES

Dante

I SCREAM up to the house, but I know what I'm going to find before I even get out of the car. My front door hangs dangerously open, warm light pouring onto the lawn I spent so much of my goddamn life, so much goddamn money keeping within HOA-approved lengths. That doesn't stop me from leaping out of the driver's seat, engine still running, and sprinting inside.

Ben stares up at me, a grinning death's head. One bullet hole, in the middle of his throat. A distant part of my brain registers that they had to get close, that it's a quick death.

The rest of me shouts, "Eleni?"

I expect the silence, but it's like stepping in front of an oncoming train. The pain doesn't hurt any less because I know it's coming. My breath turns ragged, scraping in and out of my throat as I step over Ben's corpse.

The next trail of blood leads me to the front sitting room and Andrea. Fuck. Another throat shot, like a signature. My head of house, the only woman keeping me alive before Eleni, weeps blood onto the pure white carpet she always nagged the maids to keep clean.

But she's not Eleni. Monstrously, that is a comfort.

I tear through the house. Not even another corpse to greet me. Just one rumpled carpet in the hall leading to our bedroom, spattered with a few droplets of blood. I fall to my knees in front of them, my heart hammering loud enough to drown out an army of Russians approaching to kill me. This isn't enough blood for her to be dead. Even the small pool I uncover when I straighten out the rug looks like a minor gunshot. That thought throbs in my shoulder, reminding me of the injury I haven't even checked yet. I continue to ignore it.

They took her. Eleni's gone. Seb is dead on some no-name street in the meat-packing district, and Tony probably still sits next to him, snarling at anyone who tries to touch the body. The whine of emergency vehicles cuts through my own heartbeat, reminding me Piacere is on fire across the island.

There's no other answer. The Russians have been fucking planning this. If Cal's call can be trusted, this isn't just about the Saints, either. They bided their time, and now they're swinging on the whole city at once. I won't be surprised if it turns out triad blood is flowing in Chinatown right now.

And I'm wasting my fucking time. Robotically I stand and march downstairs to my office. It's pristine, untouched, and that makes me even angrier. They don't give a fuck about whose world this is. They're just here to get rid of us.

I sit down at my computer, nearly lose it fighting through the protections Eleni put on my laptop, and begin placing calls.

"CHECK IN WHEN YOU HEAR ANYTHING." I hang up and set my phone down. The very last of the Saints' men, on probation and otherwise, has been dispatched to find Eleni. Mikey and the rest of the guys at the warehouse can handle that. I pull Ben and Andrea out of their own blood and line them up in the kitchen, where the mess will be easier to clean, then shut both their eyes. My shoulder begs for my attention, so finally, I go to the downstairs bathroom, shed my shirt, and look at myself in the mirror.

The white tank top underneath my button-down drips red. Seb's blood, mine, Ben's, Andrea's, more Russians than I can count. My shoulder oozes a fine crust of the stuff over a deep flesh wound. The bullet didn't stick in my arm, but it looks like somebody bored a gouge from my flesh with a fat, permanent marker.

I yank a bottle of isopropyl alcohol El insisted on having for every floor of the house out of the cabinet, splash it on the wound, and bite back a scream. Then, I tear the sleeve off my button-down and tie it around my upper arm. Good enough. My phone vibrates.

Sal, a local kid with a few computer classes under his belt that I picked up to run security for my house. No words, just a video link. I tap it.

In grainy, greenish black-and-white, I watch with growing nausea as a team of three masked men tear through my perimeter guards, knock on my front fucking door, and then tear through the inside of my house. The perspective switches a few times, jumping between cameras like Sal took the fucking time to cut this together. I'll bash his head against the wall for that tomorrow.

For now, my hands shake as Eleni on the video gets spotted by the team. She's unarmed, and I bite back a string of curses that I haven't installed secret weapons caches in every room. They catch her quickly. The fight is brief, but violent. I wince when they shoot her hand, and again when they hit her with the baseball bat. The blood-stains upstairs snap into perfect clarity. Then, they put a bag over her head, bring her outside, and disappear off the cameras.

Eleni is gone. I wait for the lava-rush of rage, but it doesn't come. Instead, a hard, icy calm steals over my skin. The Russians have my fiancée. Fine. I'll simply do whatever it takes to get her back. They don't know what kind of man they're messing with.

Honestly, I'm not sure I do anymore.

The emergency sirens still whine, so I turn and march back to my running car.

When I pull up to Piacere, the street crawls with firefighters and cops. The patches on the boys in blue declare them members of the 121st, the precinct I own, so I ignore them. This time, I shut off the car before climbing out.

No sooner have my feet hit the ground than Gianna sprints over, a metallic shock blanket crinkling around her. She abandons it to throw her arms around me.

"Dino," she sobs. Somehow, the childhood nickname makes sense on her lips right now. Soot lines her face, and when I hold her, she's shaking like a leaf.

I want to ask how she is. Instead, I say, "El?"

"Not here." Gianna draws a shuddering breath. "Not that I saw, or anyone else. God, people died! Crystal, she—she—"

I squeeze my cousin and watch firefighters pour water onto the smoldering wreck of everything I've built. The basement should be fireproof. But there's fireproof, and there's Russian fireproof.

One of the cops, a detective in a suit, pulls away from the group and walks our way. My arms tighten around Gianna as I recognize him. Not a fucking detective. Henry goddamn Alcott.

I release her quickly, and she stumbles away, but I barely notice as I stride over to him. My fist cocks back and flies before I finish the thought. His head snaps back, and that nose he always goddamn claimed came from the Bellini side cracks like music to my ears.

"Back up," I spit.

He pulls out a handkerchief—a fucking handkerchief!—and blots his nose. "Good to see you too. I was going to ask you if this was the fucking Russians, dickhead."

That catches me for a split second, stilling my fist before I knock out a few of his teeth for good measure. "Why?"

"Because I've been hunting their boss for months now." He presses the handkerchief to his nose and holds it there with a wince. "But I can't get the traction I need in the local syndicates. Any idea why that might be?"

I turn to Gianna. "Leave."

She blinks. Ash runs down her face like mascara. She looks from me, to Alcott, and back again.

"He's a cop," she says numbly. "I was going to warn you. He was asking around."

A spurt of anger crashes through the ice in a single hot burst. He was in my club. But it freezes over just as quickly.

"*Leave*," I repeat.

She shakes her head and storms away like she can't believe me. I turn back to Alcott.

"If you're making an offer, make it," I say.

He raises an eyebrow. "I'll admit, I thought this would be harder. But fine. Will you help me take down the Russians?"

The ice wraps jagged fingers around my bones, my muscles. I've lost almost everything. Friends, business, staff. All I have left is my honor. My father impressed into me, over and over again, that in this business, all a man has is his honor, but as long as he has that, he's more man than monster.

The video of Eleni going limp as the bat cracked into her skull plays through my mind again.

"What do you need from me?" I ask.

50

SWIMMING WITH THE FISHES

Eleni

MY STOMACH ROILS. The surface underneath me bumps and rolls. My head aches, and my hands scream with pain so loud I'm forced to open my eyes just to see what happened to them.

The world around me swims together in pieces. Dark walls, lined with something textured. Sound-proofing? No, it's hard plastic. The carpet under my cheek is equally plasticky. Something smells like gasoline, and for a single horrifying second, I think I'm back in the basement of Frank Lombardi's garage, and this has all been a dream. Then, my hand pulls my attention again, and I shock back to now.

With aching slowness, I drag my hand up until I can see it. A makeshift bandage rings my palm, soaked through with something red. No, I know what that is. Blood.

My blood.

The ground bumps again, and something moves in my vision other than me. A vision in white, totally distinct from the black of the walls and the red that is all I can understand about myself. I blink a few times, and the vision resolves.

Camila. She's wearing a set of white coveralls, but they're so stylishly cut and fitted that they seem more like a playful concession than anything actually protective. Still, she's braided her hair up into a crown around her head, so maybe she cares a little.

Nausea sinks burning fingers into my throat. Why is Camila here? Where is here? I try to ask, but only manage to moan.

"Lovely to have you in the land of the living once more." She laughs musically. "I was terribly afraid I had my boys go to all the trouble of keeping you alive, and you were so weak you managed to die anyway."

Something hums at the bottom of my hearing. It's constant, steady. Wheels! Like a car on a fairly—we hit another bump—somewhat well-paved road. I'm in a car. With Camila. Where's Ben?

"Whuh?" I manage.

She sits on something slightly above me, a bench, and pushes me onto my back with a single stiletto. Falling makes the pain in my head almost loud enough to compete with my hand.

"Don't worry, darling, I'm just taking out the trash." She smiles. "Hand?"

Hand. I have one of those. But—a few more memories swim back into place—I don't like Camila. Weakly, I try to tuck my hands away. Her light eyes harden.

"I've been very polite," she says. "I played nice with you in public. I waited for him to realize he was wasting his time. I even told the Russians I didn't want to play ball with their whole 'burn down the Saints' scheme."

That definitely hits some memory buttons. I have to warn Dante. I struggle to sit up. I have to—

She shoves me back down with her foot. "But I'm done with that. You've had your fun, but Dante is *mine*."

A weak laugh bubbles from my lips, and I manage to string a few thoughts together through the haze. "We're…engaged."

She snarls. "An impulse decision! Or something you did, with your little coed tits-and-ass routine. Do you think I didn't see right through you? I know what a gold digger looks like."

My retort that it takes one to know one doesn't make it to my mouth. That's fine. Camila is off on a tear now, gesturing wildly.

"All that time as a goddamn socialite, just trying to make him jealous." She huffs. "Spending his money, showing up in the society columns every week I could manage it, just waiting for him to check in. Do you have any idea how much fucking work that was?" She meets my gaze and shakes her head in frustration like I'm a friend she's venting to. "Those people are so goddamn stupid."

I try to focus through the waves of pain that wrack my body. Past Camila, I can just make out the shape of what looks like a front seat, with a driver and passenger. Both broad-shouldered. And if we're in a vehicle, the back here is huge. It must be a van. A few things roll past me as we whip into a turn. A pair of scissors, glistening sharp. A silencer. A half-empty bottle of vodka. Nothing I can think my way into a plan with because I'm not even bound, just held down with the weight of my own immovable body.

"And then you waltz in!" she nearly shrieks. "You bat those doe eyes, and he's putty in your hand. Years of effort for nothing. God, if I'd known he liked virgins, I'd have gotten fucking born again."

No one would believe Camila as a virgin. Certainly not the wild-eyed, ranting woman in front of me now. The van jerks to a stop, and I tumble forward, hitting every ache and bruise as I go. Camila huffs and squats next to me.

"Well, he's about to remember how good he fucking had it." She grabs my tracking necklace and yanks.

I yelp as the thin chain snaps.

"Did that hurt?" She pouts for a second, then drops it for a scowl. "Good. I used to be his. I know all his goddamn tricks."

She grabs my hand and, with a few twists, rips off my engagement ring. Something tears in my chest, alongside the broken rib.

"Maybe he'll search the whole Hudson for you." She smiles, sharp and cruel. "After all, a good man like Dante couldn't abandon your body to the fishes. He always buries his Calimerises, right?"

Before my thick tongue can shape an answer, she flings open the back door of the van, steps out, and slams it shut again. Quiet falls.

The engine rumbles softly, idling, but from where I slid to, I can't even see if there are still people in the front seat. I'm just alone in the dark.

My stomach twists. Bile coats my throat. I barely have time to twist onto my side before I vomit on the plastic carpet. The sharp movement sends pain radiating through my body. Darkness reaches into the edges of my vision. In a strangely faraway voice, someone prays Dante knows Camila as well as she knows him. Or maybe I just think that.

Everything goes black.

Thank you for reading! Claimed by the Mafia King: Mafia Kings Book 3 *starts now! Read chapter 1 next.*

CLAIMED BY THE MAFIA KING
CHAPTER 1: TOMORROW AND EVERY DAY AFTER

Eleni

I roll over in the thin cot, my whole body aching, and stare blearily at the dull gray ceiling.

The crack in one corner looks like it might've grown another millimeter since I last checked. Not that I know how long it's been.

There are no windows in here and just one heavy, metal door without even one of those little, barred windows you always see in movies to give me a clue what time it is. Camila dropped me off days or hours or months ago, and I haven't seen her since. I push myself up to sit, intending to do whatever kind of exercise I can in here to pass the time or keep in shape for whatever empty opportunity I get.

So far, all opportunities have been met with beatings. Bruises collect on my body between bright incisions where the edge of a nightstick or gun caught me.

My stomach twists. I lurch to my feet, stumble a few steps, and fall to my knees in front of the flat approximation of a toilet they allow me in here, the only furniture other than my cot. My breakfast—or lunch, or dinner—splatters noisily against the plastic. I've grown used to the burn of bile. They feed me the same food for every meal, and whatever it is, it doesn't seem to agree with me. I wipe my mouth on the increasingly stained sleeve of my shirt and slump against the floor.

In my mind's eye, I picture the diner upstate Dante took me to that one day. The food I ordered was good, but I'm craving something Dante pointed out to me on the menu called disco fries. Thick, brown gravy drenches the potatoes, dripping off the half-melted mozzarella cheese curds. I wasn't brave enough to order them last time. Now, they make my mouth water with want.

Fuck, I might actually be losing it.

With effort—more every day, though I'm trying not to think about that—I imagine Dante's face. The hard planes of his cheeks and jaw. The darkness of his eyes that rivals the night sky. His matching hair, and the soft curls in it he tries to hide like they betray a secret softness to him. Tired worry and anger floods my veins. I don't know how long I've been here, I don't know how I'm getting out, but I know that I am. Between Dante and I, no one in the world could keep me forever.

The door creaks open, and I lean up on my elbow slowly in fear of pissing off my stomach again. It grumbles but doesn't formally revolt. A broad, clean-cut guard I haven't seen before steps in with the usual plastic lunch tray of food. He takes in my position on the floor, then the reeking mess in the "toilet."

"I can come back, if you're too sick now," he says.

I blink. That's…not how this usually goes. More often than not, a heavily tattooed, Russian-accented man tosses the tray on the floor, sending the bread sliding away and spilling some of the water on the pale chicken in the middle, regardless of how pathetic I've looked. They never offered to come back. This guy doesn't even really sound like he has an accent.

"Uh, no," I say, more to keep him in the room than anything else. Despite the fact my trays have no more cutlery than a thin paper cup, every single guard has watched me eat, like I could craft a weapon from rotisserie chicken and white bread.

I already would have, if I could.

He sets the tray down and backs up a few feet. I scuttle over to it. I don't even want to picture myself anymore. The well-dressed, recently groomed version of myself Gianna and I invented is long dead. I must look feral as I tear into the chicken with my hands and wash it down with sips of the glass of water they provide with every meal and no other time. The food might be what's making me sick, but with all my throwing up, I'm nearly constantly ravenous. I can't miss the opportunity to gain any strength I can.

"How are you?" the guard asks.

I laugh, my mouth full. Mama would be horrified. The guard just nods.

"I guess that's fair enough."

A heavy curtain of silence falls between us. I glance up at him from time to time, both waiting for him to pull a weapon and yank away the slim veneer of comfort he offers, and try to figure out what the hell he is.

He wears the same clothes as the Russians, mostly. But his wife beater bears fewer stains, and his track pants don't scrape against each other with the same plastic shriek.

His sneakers…God, I could really be losing my mind, but they look like they're made of two different shoes. From my angle below him on the floor, I can see thick, unworn soles that contrast the wear of the tops and laces.

A gun juts casually out of his waistband, and a heavy club I've seen cops use dangles out of his pocket, but he doesn't reach for either of them. I have no clue what's happening, but I can't really make things worse. The bruises from my last few attempts to learn anything keep gathering friends no matter what I do.

"What day is it?" My voice is a rasp that almost scares me.

He wets his lips. "I can't tell you."

"What's your name?" I try instead.

"Yagdash." He smiles. The word sounds strange in his mouth, like the corners and angles of it don't quite fit.

"I don't believe you," I mutter before cramming the last of my slice of bread into my mouth.

Either he didn't hear me, or he doesn't want to respond. Both are fine with me. My frantic mind spins out on the possibility he's some capo I haven't met, an agent of Dante's sent to save me. I can't blow his cover. Or—I glance up at "Yagdash"—someone from the Irish Kings, or the triads. Another organization trying to swoop in while I'm vulnerable. The way he clips his words could be hiding another accent, but he looks too white for the triads to allow him membership.

If I keep my mind sharp, even as my body dissolves around me, I might survive this. And I have to survive long enough for the escape I know is coming.

"You didn't finish your chicken," Yagdash says evenly.

I glance at the completely empty tray. Not even a drop of water remains. With a scowl, I grab the plastic and flip it upside down to prove him wrong.

My heart leaps. There, scratched on the back of weak plastic, sit two words. *Hang on.*

"Ah, can't be doing that." Yagdash grabs the tray, the cup that fell off it, and the full "toilet," then leaves the room without another word.

When the metal door slams shut behind him, I lean against the side of my cot and dig my nails into my palms. Hang on. Just a little longer.

Find Claimed by the Mafia King: The Mafia Kings Book 3 here!

ALSO BY BELLA MOONDRAGON

The Alpha King's Breeder series:

Bought by the Alpha: The Alpha King's Breeder Book 1

Loved by the Alpha: The Alpha King's Breeder Book 2

Lost by the Alpha: The Alpha King's Breeder Book 3

Luna of the Alpha: The Alpha King's Breeder Book 4

Legacy of the Alpha: The Alpha Kings's Breeder Book 5

Daughter of the Alpha: The Alpha King's Breeder Book 6

Descendants of the Alpha: The Alpha King's Breeder Book 7

Shadow of the Alpha: The Alpha King's Breeder Book 8

Son of the Alpha: The Alpha King's Breeder Book 9

The Luna's Vampire Prince series:

The Culling

The Kingdom

The Conquered

Pregnant With Four Alphas' Babies

Chosen As the Breeder

Mated to Four Alphas

Threats Against the Breeder

At War for the Breeder

The Stolen Breeder

Four Alphas, Four Babies

Becoming the Luna Queen

Descendants of the Breeder

Desired by the Devil series

Whispers of the Devil

Banter of the Devil (releases 10/15/2024)

The Mafia Kings series

Indebted to the Mafia King

<u>Loved by the Mafia King</u> (releases 9/15/2024)

Claimed by the Mafia King (releases 11/15/2024)

Sign up for Bella's newsletter here.

Follow Bella on Facebook here.